War of the Gods

By

Alan Hotchkiss

A special thanks to those of you involved in making my manuscript ready for publishing. You know who you are. From cover design to editing, I couldn't have it without you. So once again, thank you very much.

Chapter 1

No one knew it at the time, but when the power went out around the planet on the 21st of March 2031, Earth would never be the same again.

This was no simple blackout that could be fixed by the usual means. This blackout would not be fixed at all, at least not by humans. And when I say the power went out, I mean the power went out on everything!

Phones, televisions, computers, cars, trains, boats and even planes. Anything that used any kind of mains electricity or battery power ceased working in the blink of an eye. Planes began to crash all over the world as they lost the use of many of their control systems. No power to engage hydraulic landing equipment, no way of contacting control towers or other aeroplanes, and with hundreds of thousands of flights suddenly descending from the skies at the same time, the result was only going be one thing, disastrous.

Many lives were lost that day and shock and panic rippled across the globe. How could this be possible? What had caused this catastrophic failure? The human race had become so reliant on electrical devices, to be suddenly without them was like being thrown back into the dark ages.

They told themselves it must just be a fault, a bad one of course, but just a fault nonetheless. Something that could and would be fixed soon enough.

However, as the days began to pass by with no sign of anything being resolved, fear and anger soon replaced shock and panic as the looters and rioters moved in.

Cities began to burn in their wake and the death tolls rose as people armed themselves for protection and took action when necessary. The army was sent out to help law enforcement gain control of the streets once again, but after they had killed more than their fair share of suspected looters and rioters, it only worsened the already volatile atmosphere.

Banks locked their doors as people scrambled to try and withdraw cash due to card machines and the world's online banking system suddenly becoming redundant.

Two weeks was all it took. In that time, with the vast population having no easy access to food or money, it became survival of the fittest. The army and police deserted their posts to guard their own families instead, allowing all-out war to descend upon the streets.

Fourteen days without power was all it had taken to send the whole world into chaos.

And then *they* arrived!

Chapter 2

As the people of Earth imploded on the ground, the skies above turned black as if a large storm was approaching. When the black sky began to turn deep red and bright red bolts of lightning shot across it, the chaos below paused to take notice.

The blood coloured sky rumbled with a continuous deafening thunder for over an hour as the population below watched on in awe and fear. The lightning strikes had steadily begun to pull closer to each other until they eventually formed a huge spinning circle, the inner of which, had the impression of a black hole.

The spinning circle of red lightning grew larger and brighter as the thunder roared ever louder, building an enormous feeling of pressure pressing down on the Earth itself. Finally, a huge boom echoed from above, and a surging beam of pulsing red power shot down from the sky and scorched the land. The beam lasted for around thirty seconds, before suddenly disappearing.

As soon as it had, the thunder quietened, the lightning vanished and the sky began to settle back to normal.

On the ground however, things were far from normal.

Where the beam had scorched the land, now stood a figure. After thousands of years of questioning, the people of Earth finally had an answer to the question, do Gods actually exist?

Turns out they did.

Unfortunately, it just wasn't the ones they were hoping for.

Chapter 3

What happened on that fateful day was not a singular occurrence. The exact same circumstances with the red lightning storm building towards beaming a God-like figure to Earth, happened simultaneously at five locations across our planet.

Some folk say it was random, but most believe the Gods chose their locations to land on Earth, deliberately and strategically.

Each God landed within a central location of the five most populated continents in our world.

Asia

Africa

Europe

North America

and South America

In Asia, a male God named Dalip landed within the Chinese city of Beijing. In Africa, a female God named Ti'ar landed in the Nigerian city of Lagos. In Europe, the God that landed within the German city of Berlin was named Cero and gave the impression of being the leader of all the Gods.

In North America, a male God named Cranock landed in the U.S. city of Los Angeles, and in the South American city of Sao Paulo, Brazil, landed another female God named Petra.

Beautiful Petra!

She always reminded me of the ancient Egyptian Queen Cleopatra. There was the obvious similar name, but that wasn't the main reason. The main reason was that she looked very much like the fabled Egyptian Queen, or at least how I pictured her to be. The Goddess Petra, had jet black, shoulder length hair, cut short along her fringe line, similar in style to Cleopatra's. She was olive skinned, which gave her a kind of Latin American look, hence the reason she was probably chosen to land where she did.

Her eyes were hypnotic. The pupils sparkled green like glittering emeralds and were always complimented with deep black eyeliner that travelled beyond her eye lines towards her temples. Gold coloured eye shadow rounded off the whole Queen Cleopatra look.

She was beautiful and I'm not ashamed to admit I found her mesmerizing. It was unfortunate that she just happened to be viewed upon as the coldest and most ruthless God of them all. Over the years, Petra was accountable for hundreds of thousands of human lives, which tends to take the shine off your boyhood crush. She wasn't alone in that respect however. Every single God was accountable for similar amounts of human lives.

Of course, when they first landed, no one knew what lay ahead for the human race.

Chapter 4

We call them Gods for two reasons, but no one knows for sure whether they really are or not. Firstly, that's how they refer to themselves, and have made it crystal clear they expect us to treat them as such. Secondly, they are either Gods or aliens much superior to humans, who kill without a second thought. There wasn't much of a queue forming to argue the case against them.

Upon appearing out of the vast laser beams that shot down from the sky, crowds began to form around the figures, with curiosity outweighing their fears. The Gods stood silent and motionless initially, perhaps to allow the crowds before them to grow, which they did rapidly.
Suddenly television screens that had been blank and powerless for weeks, burst into life across the planet.
Cero's face, the God that had landed in Europe, was now displayed on every television, monitor, laptop, tablet and phone around the globe. Anything that had a display screen, now showed the image of Cero. As he began to speak, the world fell silent to hear what he had to say.

'Citizens of Earth. For centuries you have looked to the skies and prayed to your many different Gods. Today, those prayers have finally been answered. We five, are your true Gods. From this day forth, you will worship only us and us alone. I am Cero.'
Images of the other four Gods flashed onto the screens now as Cero named them.

'Ti'ar……………….Cranock……………….Dalip……
……………..and Petra!

Follow us, work hard for us and worship us.

Please your Gods, and repent for your sins.

We gave you life. We gave you freedom. We gave you the world and how did you re-pay our kindness? Our generosity?

Let me tell you. You took the gift we gave you and destroyed it with your greed and pettiness, and your disloyalty.

You bled the planet dry of its resources all in the name of greed. Greed for so called wealth. You sucked out the core of the very thing that allowed you to live, to the point of almost destroying it altogether. You spawned like a disease across the planet, unable to contain yourselves, even when the population surpassed the amount of resources it could produce to survive. People died, yet you still continued your onslaught of spawning endlessly.

Rather than work together, you chose war. Non-stop wars, all over the planet, usually because of greed and pettiness.

If it's war you like then we will teach you all about war!'

The optimism and excitement of the crowds gathered, and those watching on screens everywhere else, were vanishing fast. Worried faces began exchanging looks with one another.

'We gave you life. The greatest gift of all, and you chose to mock us in return by praying to false Gods. Sending your thanks and misplaced gratitude everywhere bar where it should have been going. Our patience with your constant fighting, greed, pettiness and destruction of the planet is finally over. We cannot watch from afar any longer and you cannot be trusted to be left alone.

Today is the dawn of a new era.

Embrace it...........................or die!'

Chapter 5

'Fuck off back to where you came from,' broke the silence of the stunned crowd, immediately before the noise of rapid gunfire cracked through the air.

Earth's reply to Cero and the other Gods was immediate and deafening. Anyone and everyone with a weapon in the near vicinity of one of the five Gods, opened fire upon them. The ferocity of the attack, began to kick up so much smoke and dirt, Cero disappeared from sight. A full five minutes later, once the gunfire finally ceased and the smoke dispersed, Cero continued to stare down at the crowd, completely unhurt, and with a wry grin forming on his face.

'Wrong answer, but sadly unsurprising. You will now learn your place in this new world the hard way.'

As the wary crowd started to back off from the God, he held his right hand out, and watched as it became engulfed in a bright blue flash momentarily. When the flash disappeared, his hand now gripped a large and rather deadly looking weapon. It was crafted in the shape of a 'D' with the long straight, forming the handle and the curved part being made of a wide, gleaming, sharp metal.

Cero then leapt from the raised steps where he had been standing, whipping down towards the crowd in the blink of an eye. The glistening metal began to slice through bodies at a furious rate. Cero moved so quickly, it was hard to pin down where he was, but easy to tell where he had been with the trail of blood and bodies left in his wake. When he moved, it appeared as if he turned to smoke, such was the trail the blur left to the human eye.

At one point he paused, only to let go of his weapon which took off slicing through bodies on its own as it arced around like a boomerang, before landing back within Cero's grip. Finally satisfied at his killing spree he returned to the steps he had stood on before and began to address the planet once more.

'Today will be but a small demonstration of the power we possess. We are Gods and you are but slaves to us. You may not realise it yet, but you will quickly learn your place in our new world.'

Another blue flash and Cero's weapon disappeared from his grip. He then raised both his hands and held them just above head height, with his palms facing the sky, a wry grin settling on his face. Thunder rumbled high above and bolts of giant green lasers shot out of the clouds and ripped through many of the nearby buildings with catastrophic effect.

The resulting explosions completely destroyed the buildings hit directly and many of the neighbouring ones too.

The laser bombing reigned down all over the planet for nearly a full hour, reducing every major city and building in the world to rubble, and causing a loss of life on a scale never seen before. The same scenario played out where each of the other four Gods had landed, with an individual display of power before the laser bombardment from the sky commenced.

All of them able to move in the same manner as Cero and inflict death and mayhem in the blink of an eye. The only difference was that each God had their own choice of weapon and therefore used them in slightly differing styles.

However, the end result was all the same. When the devastating laser bombardment finally ended, the live feed that had continued to run the whole time, focussed on Cero once again.

'Citizens of Earth, you have deservedly suffered our wrath today. But we are not just vengeful or spiteful Gods. We can be kind and merciful too and to show that, we will now allow you some time to come to terms with what has happened today. Time that will allow you to mourn if need be, to bury loved ones and then re-adjust and prepare yourself to be ready to move forward, on what will be our New Earth. In three days we will make another broadcast with instructions for you. Listen carefully, and do as we say or you will face our wrath with even more fury than you have witnessed today.'

The broadcast then went dead. It's estimated that the landing day attack wiped out half of the population of Earth, which would have worked out at around four billion lives.

Chapter 6

Three days later

When screens across the globe suddenly burst into life again, Cero's smirking face addressed the surviving half of the population.

'Welcome to the dawn of a new era for the planet of Earth. The era of the Gods. Together we will now re-shape this planet into one befitting of its rulers. This will be done using our knowledge and human labour. If you work hard and obey our laws, you will be rewarded with accommodation, food, clothing and general necessities. Money, jewels, gold, silver, anything that once represented wealth and greed in your old society is now worthless. It has no place in our New Earth. The only way to move forward in life now, is to work and obey. Please your Gods, and you will find reward and fulfilment. Disappoint, or disobey us, and you will find certain death. There is no room on our Earth for the weak, lazy, greedy or dishonest amongst you. If you are such, you will not last long.

Do not be sad, move on from your old lives. Our New Earth will be glorious.

As you will have noticed, we have the ability to control all the power sources on Earth. We took the power away, fourteen days before we arrived, and we can restore it anywhere we choose in the blink of an eye. You can live in our world with light and comfort or choose to run and hide in fear and darkness.

The remainder of your many different armed guards across the planet have already readily agreed to be part of our New Earth and so, we have restored the power to many of their vehicles and such.

Starting from dawn tomorrow, the various armed services will begin trawling the land, looking for survivors and humans ready to embrace their Gods and our new world. Make your way to any road or highway and await collection from the armed services. From there you will be transported to special holding areas where we will determine what skills you have and what best way they can be utilised for you to serve your Gods and help build our New Earth.

This collection will run for seven days. After this time, anyone that has not made themselves available for pick up and sworn their loyalty to the Gods, will be declared an enemy of the New Earth. The punishment for this and opposing the Gods will be certain death. We do not give second chances.

We are not weak and corrupt like the past rulers of all your nations. Your so called justice systems and laws did more for those who broke them, than what they did to uphold them. Our laws will be absolute, and if you break them, you won't live to do it again. It's no wonder the world turned into the mess it did, under the guidance of these lying, greedy and corrupt pieces of human filth.'

As the broadcast of Cero began to zoom out from the God, a row of men and woman on their knees, with their hands tied behind their backs, quickly came into view behind him. Each and every one of them, instantly recognisable as the leaders of their various nations. The prime ministers, presidents, chancellors, kings and queens of most of the European countries such as the United Kingdom, Germany, France, Spain and Russia were all present in the line-up.

'Each and every human being on this planet had a part to play in leading us to this point. Not as large a role however, as each and every one of these so called leaders behind me. Unlike most of you, they actually had the power to change things. Stop petty wars, stop draining the planet of its nutrients, stop famines, eradicate disease, and help the poor. But they chose not to. They chose to continue the trend of greed and corruption and to turn a blind eye to all of the problems of the planet. Today, as a symbol of change, they will pay the price of their actions.'

As the camera moved up and down the European leaders, many of them were whimpering and crying and begging for mercy.

'Look at the sorry state of these so called leaders before me. Leaders are supposed to be strong and brave, even in death. Do these weak individuals represent leaders? And before you all begin to blame this sorry lot for your troubles, think again. What does this say about all of you? That you were all content and happy to be ruled over, to be bent and broken and bullied by such a bunch of weak and disgusting human beings.'

Silence fell as Cero stared angrily into the camera. The look on his face said it all.

After a moment or two, he turned suddenly and outstretched his right arm. A flash of blue light sparkled in the air, before Cero's weapon appeared in his hand, humming quietly as a charge of blue light pulsed up and down the blade.

The cries and whimpers of the leaders grew louder and louder before being silenced altogether as a blur flashed by them. A thump, thump, thump, was heard as one by one, each of the now ex-European leaders' detached heads landed on the ground.

The camera slowly moved along the line of bodies, ensuring that everyone watching across the globe could see in great detail, exactly what had happened to the former European leaders. After a solemn minute or two, the camera returned to Cero.

'This was not meant as a demonstration of power, rather a symbolic gesture. A gesture to help you all forget what once was and to focus you on the future of our New Earth. Pay attention and absorb this gesture.'

The live feed then blacked out for a moment before returning, only this time, the face that adorned the screen was a vision of beauty. The Goddess Petra stared sullenly into the screen as it panned out to reveal her standing in front of a line of men and women just as Cero had been. This time the line was made up of powerful South American leaders. Not just politicians however, major drug cartel bosses made the line up as well.

As Petra continued to stare sullenly into the screen, you couldn't not be taken in by her beauty. She looked mean and sullen and dangerous, but above all, utterly beautiful. The sultry image quickly vanished when Petra crossed her hands over her body and appeared to pull two golden daggers from either side of her, despite there being no sign of them moments ago.

The golden daggers were Petra's weapon of choice and were designed in a kind of angled teardrop shape, sweeping outwards from the rounded handle in a curving blade. The whole dagger, including the bladed part was made from the same golden material and when used, appeared to light up with a blue light, similar to Cero's.

And just like the leader of the Gods, Petra soon put her daggers into action, as she swept up and down the line of people, removing more heads from their body. It was done so quickly you would be forgiven for thinking she hadn't moved at all as she stared sullenly into the camera once more from the exact same spot she had seconds ago.

The screens turned black again before returning to another God. This time it was Cranock's turn.

For all that Petra was sullen and silent, the North American God appeared loud and brash. Cranock's choice of weapon was a rather strange club like object. It was made of a very dense silver metal, in the shape of a thick baseball bat. Yet rather than a rounded end it had a strange design, much like that of a castle's turret. It was crude and lethal, as was the God that wielded it.

Although he was capable of moving at high speed like the other Gods, Cranock walked slowly up and down the line of North America's most powerful people, mocking and yelling at them. He then paused at the end of the row and smiled at the camera before swinging his club at the head of his nearest victim, which just happened to be the president of the United States of America.

The movement was effortless for Cranock, hardly even much of a swing, yet when his weapon hit the back of the president's head, it pulverised it into a thousand pieces.

Those watching around the world could see exactly what was happening this time. Just as Cranock wanted. He made his way through the rest of the line, slowly pulverising each victim, one by one, covering the room in blood and brain matter in the process.

After working his way through them all, he looked at the camera and signed off with another smile and mock salute.

From there, next up was the Goddess in Africa, Ti'ar, who made quick work of the row of leaders and power brokers from that area of the world. Ti'ar was beautiful to look at too, albeit in a differing way from Petra. Her hair was short, her skin dark and she was more of an imposing figure than Petra, taller and more athletically built. She moved with the prowess of a Lion ready to strike at its prey.

Ti'ar's weaponry of choice were two swords that she kept secured on her back with a handle protruding over each shoulder. The swords were made from an unknown material and were jet black in colour. When used they fizzed with a purple coloured type of energy. You had to admit they were two of the finest blades ever to be seen. It was just unfortunate that it meant an untold amount of humans would be getting chopped into pieces for the pleasure of seeing these fine weapons in action.

If ever there was a good time to view them, then this was it. As with all the other corrupt and greedy leaders around the world, few could argue they were undeserving of this day. Of course, that didn't stop them from beginning to argue loudly to the contrary. However, Ti'ar's fine swords soon quietened their voices with a slick and lethal display that ended with yet more heads detached from bodies and the floor awash with blood.

For the final broadcast that day, the cameras now moved to the God in Asia. Dalip was oriental in appearance, which again suggests where the Gods landed was not co-incidental.

Dalip wasn't a brash talker like Cranock. His style was more sly, agile and cunning. When Dalip was about to dish out some vengeance, two silver sticks would appear in each hand, as if they had just slid out of his sleeves. The sticks of silver would then appear to almost melt as they grew thinner and extended downwards until each stick had developed into a long gleaming whip.

These whips were vicious instruments that had the power to slice through concrete as if it were butter. Yet Dalip was also capable of using them with a much more delicate effect if and when required. For example, he could slice a man's head off if he wanted or with the exact same whip, he could just as easily use it to wrap around a man's leg or waist without doing any damage to him other than restraining him. However, if you found yourself in this position and were thinking at least he wasn't going to kill you, the whips had another surprise up their sleeves, so to speak.

As the end of the whip was wrapped around you, thinner strips of the liquid mercury-like material would suddenly grow out from the main whip and end in razor sharp points or claws or whatever shape Dalip wanted it to. These smaller extensions of the main whips could just as easily kill you as the main part could and more often than not they were indeed used to kill, just in a slower, more painful manner than the larger whip would do the job. As some of Asia's most powerful men and woman were about to find out.

A flick of his right wrist sent one of Dalip's gleaming whips surging towards the row of people before him. A loud crack was heard as the first four casualties' heads were detached from their bodies in the blink of an eye.

Before the heads had even hit the ground, Dalip's other whip had wound itself around the next two men in the line-up, before squeezing them together tightly. Countless smaller wires began to grow out of the main whip now. Two of the smaller extensions that ended in small claw like hooks, shot into one of the men's eyes, then whipped backwards again, pulling free his eyeballs and leaving him screaming in horror.

Another of the extensions that moulded into a razor sharp blade, began to slice and dice the other man. It sliced off both his ears, then his scalp, his nose, eyebrows, even his lips were mutilated by this precise razor. It then proceeded towards his body, slicing up and down and across until it became such a bloody mess it was impossible to tell what it was doing to him anymore.

Their horrifying torture was brought to end with another flick of Dalip's wrist, which pulled the main whip tight and sliced through the two bodies like cheese wire. The rest of his victims died in similar manners. The lucky ones, if you could call them that, were those that had their heads sliced off quickly by the main whip. The rest suffered rather more before coming to their own bloody end. Dalip's whips were probably the most horrifying weapons out of the five Gods.

Once the execution was over, the whips dissolved back into two seemingly harmless looking metal sticks, before disappearing up Dalip's sleeves.

Finally the screens went dark again. Not many humans were left needing any more displays of power from the Gods after the devastation of their landing day. However, for the odd few that remained in doubt, they didn't anymore. From dawn the next day, landing day survivors around the world began to make their way towards highways and main roads for collection, to begin their new life serving the five Gods.

Chapter 7

Over the following weeks and months, humans were collected by trucks and buses and taken to specially built holding areas for cleaning, immunisation, evaluation and to learn the new laws and rules the Gods had set for them. Once evaluated, they were designated their new role and sent to different areas for clothing and to learn what would be expected of them in their particular positions, and the punishment if they did not fulfil their duties.

The designated roles more or less fell under five groups, cooking, cleaning/maintenance, building, medical and the armed forces. Eyebrows were raised at the vast amount of numbers that were being designated for the armed forces. Why the need for such large armies across the world when the Gods held all the power? We would find out the answer to that soon enough.

With money now being a thing of the past, what you received in return for your service to the Gods was survival. You earned a roof over your head and three square meals a day. There were no more supermarkets to go and buy your weekly shopping or fast food joints to pig out on junk food. No fancy restaurants to spoil yourself with the occasional night of fine dining or sweet shops to overindulge with.

Vast canteens were built, a bit like old fashioned soup kitchens. You reported to your nearest one, scanned your I.D. then joined the queue to collect your food. This was repeated for breakfast, lunch and dinner. If you missed any, it was tough luck, you went hungry. Slept in? Five minutes late? It didn't matter, when it shut, it shut and that was it until the next allocated meal time.

The builders' numbers nearly matched that of the armed forces to begin with, however that wasn't a surprise after the destruction of landing day. There was much to be built and most of the Gods' workforce required new accommodation.

For most workers this came in the form of small, basic units that comprised of a living room, one or two bedrooms and a toilet. The power was still controlled in some way by the Gods. They allowed lighting, be it street and internal but there wasn't much else. Each unit had a small television screen in the living room, but it was controlled by the Gods and only sprang into life when they had an announcement to convey across the land. As time passed by, these large sites of basic units soon became known as the slums.

More accommodation was built that offered varying degrees of comfort and certain workers or armed forces would be moved up from the basic units as a reward for their exemplary service or brave actions that pleased or benefited the particular God they were serving under.

However, the first and main concern for most of the builders was to construct lavish new accommodation, worthy of a God. Not that it was left up to the builders to design and build. As you can imagine, the Gods instructed the builders what they required and oversaw each project. New advanced technology was also introduced by the Gods to help such work, albeit only on a need to know basis.

Five mega-homes were built in each city where the Gods landed. I say homes but in reality they were actually more like mini cities, contained within one building. Each identical, and interestingly in the same shape as the fabled great pyramids of Egypt, except much larger.

The top third of these futuristic pyramids was the Gods' each private living area. The other two thirds was a sprawling metropolis of mysteries that few humans ever got the chance to explore. Only the most loyal and prized servants or warriors were given quarters in these great pyramids.

There was one other project that the builders were put to task on immediately that would soon involve many of the men and women from the armed forces, who, like the builders, were hard at work themselves.

The Gods had quickly taken away and destroyed most of the world's modern weaponry, ranging from small hand guns right through to nuclear bombs. They said that if human's lust for power and destruction was so strong, then they would need to earn it the hard way. For too long, tyrants and power brokers reigned terror and bloodshed upon whole countries from the comfort of a plush office, and without having to wield a weapon in anger themselves.

The Gods used themselves as prime examples of what the humans should be trying to aspire to. Any leader should be strong both physically and mentally and not expect followers to do anything they are not capable of themselves. From now on, anyone wishing to be a leader amongst the human race would have to prove they were capable and worthy. The Gods claimed humans had not advanced enough as a species to be trusted with the weaponry they had invented and created, and had continued to display a lust for fighting and bloodshed over and over, never once learning to live in peace with each other. Therefore, if they could not rid themselves of this gene, then the Gods would take them back to a time in their history when they had at least shown a form of bravery and skill in the arena and on the battlefield.

And so, began a new era of gladiators. Centuries after the form of entertainment was deemed too barbaric and uncivilised for the modern world.

The builders' already busy schedule became even busier as the Gods informed them of their plans for new colosseum type arenas to be built across the New Earth. The first and most grandiose ones would of course be built near to each of the Gods pyramid buildings.

Training camps were also built where the most promising recruits from the armed forces were sent to learn the fine art of close combat warfare with the only weapons that were still permitted by the Gods, including swords, spears, axes, daggers, and hammers. Basically, any handheld weapon that wasn't a firearm.

The fighting contests didn't start right away, with too much hard labour required building and re-shaping the Gods' vision of the New Earth. It was three years after landing day that the first modern day gladiator games commenced at Cero's colosseum, on the outskirts of the city of Berlin, Germany.

The colosseum was huge and could hold up to one hundred thousand spectators. It would have ruled the surrounding skyline had it not been for the even larger, great pyramid building in the background.

Each pyramid was the same, a modern marvel in construction. Perhaps not surprising with the Gods' power and technology however, it was still a feat to behold. With all of them finally complete, along with their accompanying colosseums, the first competition at Cero's would mark the dawn of the new gladiator era, closely followed by further competitions at all the other Gods' arenas.

Another form of blood sport that the Gods had in store for our race, was on a much grander scale.

Chapter 8

The reason for the Gods directing such huge numbers of humans into the armed forces had remained somewhat of a mystery for those first few years, even after the games began in the colosseums. Another year on from the beginning of the gladiator contests, the Gods announced that the first full scale battle would take place between two of the Gods' armies.

A date and location were set, with the number of combatants being limited to five thousand on either side. This was a war to be fought out up close and personal, in large numbers, purely for the entertainment of the Gods. Each army was led by their own champion gladiator and were warned they were fighting for the pride of their God. Losing was not an option as any surviving members of a losing army would be dealt with harshly by their own God.

To this day, no God has had to deal with their own losing army, purely down to the fact that no survivors were ever left alive by a winning army.

Viewing platforms would be erected on the location of the battles so that the Gods could watch the gory entertainment in person, whilst cameras would broadcast the live action across every television screen, within every home, ensuring all the habitants of the New Earth could see the action too, as they did with the gladiator battles in the colosseums.

Families had to endure watching their loved ones die brutal deaths from their own living rooms. It was savage and cruel and yet, very quickly became loved equally as much by the humans as it was by the Gods.

Perhaps it was a much needed vent of anger and frustration after years of hardship under the Gods rule or perhaps the Gods were right, and the human races lust for violence and power and war, was indeed insatiable.

New heroes of the human race were formed in the colosseums and then the champion gladiators would lead their Gods' army into battle. All of which appeared to mean nothing more than bragging rights between the Gods, yet still the humans embraced it.

For every single gladiator event, the colosseums around the globe were full to the max. The system for gaining entry to these events worked mostly on a random allocation. If chosen, your ticket as such would be uploaded to your i.d. card and scanned upon entry. If chosen and you didn't want to attend, you notified one of the guards on duty at the soup kitchens and your ticket would be re-allocated. There wasn't many who passed up the opportunity when selected and every event was full to capacity, which speaks for itself about the appeal the gladiatorial games had on the population. Tickets could also be allocated as rewards, if someone's actions had pleased their God.

Now all this might sound like life had become easier or more enjoyable for humans under the rule of the Gods. However, it wasn't. Life was still extremely hard and unforgiving. The gladiator/war events were the only source of entertainment and outlet humans had, so they were as popular as they were needed.

Day to day life for the human race comprised of working/serving, eating and sleeping. There was no such thing as weekends off to relax or holiday breaks to take your family on vacation. You served the Gods in whatever role you had been chosen to do, seven days a week, for fifty-two weeks of the year and were grateful for it.

The working days or nights, were long and meal breaks short. There wasn't much time for anything else anyway. Families were now restricted to having one child under the age of twelve. Once the child was over twelve years old you were permitted to have another. If a pregnancy occurred before this, you were required to report it and subsequently have it aborted. If the pregnancy was discovered before it had been reported it would be punished by having the female sterilised as well as the abortion, ending any chance of future pregnancies. On the rare occasion that an illegal pregnancy made it to birth undiscovered, when it finally came to light, the whole family, including the newly born infant, would be killed. With the parent's deaths usually being a brutally, painful and public ending.

The laws were strict and the Gods unforgiving.

The reason for the age restriction being twelve was due to the fact, this was the age when children would begin their service to the Gods. Their path would be chosen, normally following in the footsteps of their mother or father and then they would begin their working life.

Depending on what service they had been chosen for, you might be sent for training first. For example, if you were chosen for the armed forces, you would be sent to training camp with other children of a similar age for four years. Then at the tender age of sixteen you are deemed worthy of joining the ranks of the frontline armed forces or else deemed unworthy and cast off to work in the soup kitchens or become a cleaner or other less glamorous position.

It was the same with the builders, you would spend several years doing hard labour before you were even considered to be worthy of learning a specific trade. The builders were probably the hardest option for a child. At only twelve years old, you suddenly found yourself being worked into the ground for long hours, every single day of the week. It was back breaking and soul destroying. I know from first-hand experience.

Not that any of the other options were going to be much fun either for a twelve-year-old child. Whatever service you were chosen for, you were the runt. Last in and least cared about and would be handed the worst and most menial chores for the next few years of your life at least. If you were sent to be a cook, then you would be washing dishes or peeling potatoes, every single day of your life for at least four years before you even got to think about cooking anything.

If you were a cleaner, then it would be the toilet duties for you. Imagine being a twelve year old and having to clean up strangers' shit every day of your life.

The armed forces were definitely the preferred option amongst most of the male population, mainly due to the hero status of the champion gladiators. However, going in as a twelve year old, you were about as far away from being a champion gladiator as a toilet cleaner. Initial training for the armed forces was beyond tough and very quickly weeded out the weak, who were then sent elsewhere. From there, the training was violent and brutal and many deaths occurred during this period alone.

If you actually made it through training and progressed to the full ranks, death was the most likely outcome anyway, during a gladiatorial battle or a full war battle.

Only the champion gladiators or war heroes were sometimes offered positions within the great pyramids or in charge of street patrols and lived to tell their tales. However, they were few and far between.

Chapter 9

2055

Twenty five years since the Gods' landing day, I stand on the cusp of greatness. One more gladiatorial battle to win to become not only the champion, but the youngest ever to do so. The one slight problem standing in my way of destiny, is the current, undefeated champion and in some ways a hero of mine. He also happens to have a record to his name, of being the longest reigning champion in history. No small feat and a hefty challenge that lies before me.

However, before we get into that, you're probably wondering who I am? Well, my name is Jacob and my story began in 2037, six years after landing day. I was born to a builder father and cook mother. Right from birth, my options in twelve years' time did not look promising. I was raised mostly by my mother as is custom for one parent to leave their normal working duties to allow them to raise and educate their child until they turn twelve and join the working ranks. Most couples are able to choose which parent will raise the child unless one of them holds an important position and is not permitted to leave by the Gods.

From the age of four your education, or brainwashing as some would call it began. It would comprise of basic maths, writing, language skills and a hefty chunk of what rules and laws you must abide by. Your place in the world as a servant to your Gods was high on the agenda too. On the plus side, the Gods were keen to have able fit bodies to work for them, so daily exercise was compulsory and formed my favourite part of the day.

Two sessions, one in the morning and one in the afternoon were scheduled for exercise and were a great escape for the children of the settlement from the monotonous classroom type work.

The world may have been a vastly different place to what it was like before the Gods landed, however, being born after landing day, I knew no difference and the world was just the world to me and to the other children of our settlement. Therefore, looking back I would have to say I had a reasonably happy childhood. At least up until the age of twelve.

Boy did I have a rude awakening then.

Having watched many great gladiatorial battles over the years, (it was mandatory for everyone to watch them, children included) and having excelled at sports, I had hoped to follow in the footsteps of some of the great champions of the arena. However, with what appeared to be very little thought other than my father is a builder, so I'll be one too, I was chosen to enter the builders' program.

On the day of my twelfth birthday, I rose at 5am in order to get ready and leave with my father to be collected in time for our 6am start. On arrival, my father left to report to where he was working and I was sent to another part of the site where I was introduced to the crew I would be working for.

They were a small, nasty, bitter group of men, who were as unwelcoming as they were unfriendly. My attempts to say hello were met with growls and looks that could kill. The rest of my day was filled with grunt work, mostly digging and lifting until my back was agony and my hands a blistering mess. All the while, I was on the receiving end of constant yelling, kicks and shoves from this horrible group of men as uncaring guards passed by without giving it a second thought.

It was a brutal introduction to working life for an innocent twelve year old child. When our shift finished at 6pm, I nearly burst into tears upon meeting my father again. Noticing the state of me, he quickly growled into my ear, 'Stay strong boy! Don't let them see you cry, not here.'

I somehow managed to hold it together until we arrived back at our home, where I finally let all the stress and exhaustion of the day out with a flood of tears as I cuddled my mother and father.

The following morning, more tears flowed as I had to be dragged kicking and screaming from my bed at 5am. My parents cried too as they tried to explain to their child that if you didn't attend your duties you would be killed. Plain and simple.

The harsh truths of life come thick and fast when you turn twelve in this world.

When we arrived on site that day, rather than head off towards his own location, my father tried to walk with me towards my area. He never told me why, but I presume he was looking to inflict his own pain on the horrible crew I had been tasked to. We didn't get far before several guards noticed and quickly screamed for us to halt. My father tried to ignore them and press on, however a crack echoed through the air and he fell to the ground suddenly in pain.

As I gazed down, blood had already begun to seep through his shirt from the nasty gash that the guard's whip had inflicted upon him. Before I had a chance to react, I was sent sprawling forwards as another guard's large foot struck my back.

'Get on your way grunt,' growled the guard menacingly.

Scared and unsure what to do, I slowly continued on my way, glancing around at my father as I went. He looked up and caught my eye, mouthing, 'Stay strong son!' before another horrible crack filled the air and he crumbled in pain once more. I couldn't watch to see what happened after that.

The rest of day didn't fare much better as I continued to be worked into the ground, beaten and yelled at constantly. Upon finishing and meeting my father, he looked as bad as I felt and we spent the journey home suffering in silence.

The next two years were extremely hard on our family as I continued to be treated horrendously and my parents suffered the mental torture of being unable to help me. The only positive you could possibly take out of the situation was that my body had developed extremely well over the two years, with all the hard labour I was doing. My father must have noticed this too, as one night he took me aside after I had returned home with a particularly nasty looking black eye from being struck deliberately in the face with a plank of wood.

'Son, I know you're not an adult yet, but you're maturing and getting stronger every day. You'll need to fight back if you ever want this abuse to stop. They may be older and nastier looking than you, but that doesn't matter. You've grown bigger and stronger. You just need to find the confidence to stand up to them. You have the biggest heart in the world and just by showing up and doing your duties each day has shown that nothing can beat you but yourself. The next time one of them hurts you, hurt them back. But make sure you hurt them back at least twice as hard.

You do that son and trust me, they won't mess with you again. You may get punished by the guards, but it will be worth it in the long run. You're stronger than you know son.'

I'll never forget those words and I lay on my bed for the rest of the evening thinking over what my father had said. The next day when we went to part ways, he paused and put his hand on my shoulder.

'When the time comes, don't hesitate son. Use the pain they've caused you and make them suffer for it. Put them down and put them down good.'

He was growling in anger himself as he said those words, before giving me a curt nod and heading off.

As the day wore on, and my father's words from the previous evening were still running through my head, I began to look at myself and my crew in a different light. Some of them actually looked weak when I compared them to myself. They were thin and wiry, whereas I was beginning to bristle with rippling muscles. Looking back, when you suffer so much from such an early age it can be hard to actually realise you may be stronger than what you think, and even harder to do anything about it, but that day was my day and I was about to do something drastic about it.

It all started over something rather trivial, when you compare it to some of the other things that had been going on.

I had been busy mixing a bucket of mortar and was just about to take it to one of the crew when another two of them happened to be walking by. As I was bending over to lift the bucket, the youngest of the pair, a lad of around eighteen, kicked it from my grasp and sent the contents splattering over the ground and myself.

Normally I'd just have picked it up and started all over again in silence. But not today. Today I stood tall and growled some kind of profanity at the man. The pair of them immediately stopped laughing and looked at me in disbelief that I had the cheek to respond in such a manner.

'What did you say grunt?'

'You heard.'

The words had just left my lips when the lad punched me square on the chin, as he had done many, many times before. This time however, I barely flinched. A large grin then broke out on my face, because today was the first day when I actually realised his punch couldn't hurt me. There was no pain. It was so weak it barely even registered with my brain.

My reaction was definitely not what they were expecting and the commotion had now caught the attention of the rest of the crew.

The initial pairs' shock was now turning to anger at my blatant show of disobedience and the younger lad responded by landing yet another punch on my chin. This time I burst out laughing, mocking him further in front of the gathering crew. His face turned red with anger and embarrassment and he moved to send another punch in my direction. However, I was done with being the punch bag and ready to dish out some punishment of my own.

I stopped laughing, gritted my teeth and let the fury and rage that had been brewing within me for a long time, rise up.

As the young man's pathetic fist was arcing its way slowly around towards my head, in the blink of an eye I stepped closer, took aim and with all my might launched a punch of my own, and boy did it connect.

My fist smashed right into his mouth, making a loud crunching noise as bits of broken teeth flew off in every direction. The fleeting look of pain and shock resonating on the man's face, just before his eyes rolled to the back of his head and he collapsed backwards out cold, sent an enormous feeling of satisfaction rippling through my body.

I now turned my attention to the other crew member who had been with the younger man. Another bully who had tormented me daily over the last few years, from verbal abuse to hitting me with tools, rocks and even burning me with a blow torch on more than one occasion.

Older and thinner than the younger man, he resembled nothing more than a weasel to me now as he stood with his mouth open in shock, gazing at his unconscious partner.

Slowly he turned to face me, his face twisting and changing from the look of shock to one that now could only be likened to the features of an angry rat.

'Who the hell do you think you are grunt? You'll pay for that,' he spat out, before raising his right arm which happened to be holding a claw hammer, and swinging it for my head.

'Not today weasel,' I thought to myself as I ducked down to avoid the swinging hammer, then continued forward, grabbing him around his waist before hoisting him over my shoulder. I then charged forward, almost laughing as the weasel screamed in panic for me to put him down. Reaching the edge of the raised area we had been working upon, I duly granted him his wish as I heaved him off my shoulder and sent him flying over the edge. He fell about ten metres before landing painfully on top of a pile of cast off bricks and boulders. The noise his body made on impact and his subsequent non-human like moan cast no doubt he had endured some seriously painful injuries at least. Another pang of satisfaction.

Yells of profanity and 'What have you done?' from behind, quickly made me spin around.

Three more crew members were racing towards me, faces contorted with anger and rage. Staying put, next to the edge of the drop I had just sent weasel over wouldn't have been the wisest tactical decision, so instead I opted to sprint forward and meet the incoming danger head on. The closest member was tearing down to my left, making me divert to meet him first. As we neared he threw something, most likely a brick, which just narrowly avoided my head. I then slipped to the side to avoid his large fist which was now bearing down on me and instead used my momentum to slip an uppercut, clean off the underside of his chin. The punch, together with his own momentum from running towards me, sent him up into the air, before landing heavily several yards away.

The next man, learned from his comrade before him and slowed upon reaching me, developing a fighter's stance, rather than leaping in carelessly. He snarled at me, showing off a set of black, rotten molars in the process.

Two jabs stung my face in quick succession, followed by a speedy right hook. This one, had done some boxing training at least, but I was beyond pain or being hurt and the blows did nothing more than rile me further. I continued to stand with my hands by my side, laughing at the man to antagonise him further, which was working well, if the look upon his face was anything to go by. After another jab stung my face, I then planted a punch of my own on his, which had much more of an impact. He staggered back, shaken, before regrouping and advancing once more. I continued to let him hit me, yet after each punch he threw, I laughed then threw one of my own.

Several punches later, he was bent over in pain with blood pouring from his mouth. I moved in for the kill when something heavy cracked off the back of my skull.

I definitely felt the blow this time, but it failed to knock me over or do any serious damage other than sting somewhat. I snapped my head around to see another particularly nasty member of the crew standing with a broken in half shovel. Having failed to have the desired result of nailing me with a shovel, his face now bore a look of worry as he took in the look of fury upon my face.

I stepped forward quickly and unleashed a vicious kick at his private area, which caught him flush. Bellowing with pain, he buckled over, dropping what was left of the shovel in order to grab his testicles. This now left his head in a dangerous area and I was going to make him regret taking a shovel to mine. With both hands, I grabbed the back of his head then pulled it towards me, whilst at the same time bringing my knee up rapidly until it made a satisfying crunch into his face and sent him sprawling to the ground.

Just then, the boxer had recovered and grabbed me from behind, around my neck in a choke hold and was squeezing my windpipe as hard as he could. At the same time, the third crew member that had attacked me, was now back on his feet and had collected the wooden pole part of the broken shovel from the ground. As I pulled and twisted, trying to free myself of the strong arm that was squeezing tightly around my neck, the shovel pole smacked into my rib cage.

Struggling to breathe, I couldn't make out what the third man was shouting as he whacked the pole into my midriff again, but he definitely didn't appear to be happy with me. Unable to deal with him however, he continued to beat me with the pole as I struggled to free myself from the choke hold.

Looking back, it was at this point that I noticed over the shoulder of the man with the shovel handle, three guards standing not too far away, watching the action unfold before them. I didn't think much of it at the time because I only noticed them in a fleeting glance and I had enough on my plate with one man choking me and another beating with a pole. But in hindsight, it was strange on two accounts. Firstly, it was not like the guards to stand off if trouble was flaring. They usually stepped in quickly and heavy handed. Secondly, they were expected to run a tight ship by the Gods and if word got back to their superiors that things had got out of hand, the guards would find themselves facing serious repercussions. This however, was all an afterthought to me, for the time being I was more concerned with things closer to hand.

Fearing if I lost consciousness, I may never wake up again, I clawed desperately at the man's face in an attempt to free myself. As my fingers moved over his eyes, I knew I had my chance. I poked them into his eyeballs as hard as I could until they felt like they had almost pushed so far into the man's eye that I couldn't be far away from his brain, and the animal like howl that he suddenly let out, backed up my thoughts. Finally I heard a loud popping noise. I'm not sure what that meant for his eyeballs, but it did the trick for me and he released his grip around my neck just as the pole whacked into my ribs again.

My hands instinctively shot down to the retracting pole and caught hold of it before it was out of reach. The man tried to yank it free but I held on firmly before pulling on it sharply myself. The move caught him off balance and he stumbled clumsily towards me. I stepped forward and greeted his nose with my forehead, feeling it crunch under the impact. Stumbling backwards now, he relinquished the weak grip he had on the pole in order to raise his hands towards his injured nose.

With the pole now solely in my possession, I decided to let him feel its sting and swung it rapidly at the side of his head. The blow sent him to the floor, where I followed up with a vicious flurry of blows until his eyes had rolled to the back of his head and I had sustained enough damage to his face to satisfy my burning desire for revenge.

I then turned my attention to the boxer who was currently bent over, cradling his eyeballs. A blow to the back of his head, put him out of his misery.

I turned just in time to the see the first runt, who had initiated the trouble by kicking over my bucket, charging towards me. Unable to move in time, he barrelled into me, sending us both tumbling across the ground, with him finishing up on top of me. He must have thought he was going to win the fight from there, as a wicked grin flashed across his face, revealing bloodied and freshly broken teeth.

I almost laughed to myself at the thought, as my confidence was soaring and I knew nothing was going to beat me now. He raised his fist but before he could even send it down towards me, I used my strength to push him to the side, then pin him down as I rolled over and gained the advantage. He tried to now do the same to me but I was too strong for him and this time did laugh out loud at his wriggling and squealing.

A quick flurry of punches soon stopped both. However, the rage that had been burning within me for the last two years wouldn't let me stop there and I continued to rain blows down upon his bruised and bloodied face. Looking back, it's hard to say whether I would have stopped before he was dead or not, but a loud crack echoing through the air, thankfully signalled the end was nigh, whether I wanted it to be or not.

Chapter 10

'That's enough boy,' boomed a loud voice, right after the whip had cracked off the ground beside me. With my fist raised mid-air, ready to strike down, I looked up to see three guards standing about ten yards away. The three that had been watching from the start, I presumed. The middle guard, who I could see was a superior, was busy winding his whip back in. The guards on either side of him, didn't have any weapons drawn yet, but their itchy fingers were already grasping at the handles of their batons, eager to dish out a lesson of their own.

'He's had enough boy, get off him now!' said the head guard, in a loud, gravelly voice.

Despite the guards' presence, fire still raged within me and I was keen on exacting more punishment on the whole crew.

'I won't ask you again boy. Step away from the man and come with us the easy way, or throw that next punch you have lined up and you'll be coming with us the hard way. And trust me, you won't like the hard way.'

I was angry, but not completely stupid. The heavy hands of the guards were well known and to be honest, I was surprised at being given an option. I had fully expected the guards to announce their presence with a baton or whip to my head, followed by many more. This was unusual to say the least.

I lowered my fist, stood up and moved slowly away from the battered man.

'Wise choice,' said the guard. 'Now get over here boy.'

I approached the guards cautiously, still expecting to feel their wrath sooner rather than later.

'Are you going to be any trouble or can I trust you to come with me without any hassle?' asked the superior guard, once I stood before him.

'Yes sir, I won't be any hassle to you. Those men deserved everything they got but I bear no grudges towards you or your men.'

'Well lucky us then, eh?' announced the guard in between laughing with his comrades at my reply. When they finally stopped laughing he gave me a serious look and added, 'Don't make me regret this boy.'

'I won't sir.'

'Right, you two sort out this mess and you, come with me,' said the superior, nodding to his men, then signalling with his finger for me to follow him.

'You sure boss?' asked one of the guards, eyeing me with contempt.

'Yeah I'm sure, let's go.'

I followed the superior guard in silence as we crossed the large site. Many workers stopped what they were doing to gawk in wonder at what a young grunt could have done to be in such serious trouble that he was being led away by a superior.

I was grateful we didn't pass my father as I'm sure he would have tried to intervene and help his son. However, it would probably have just made matters worse for both of us.

It was my doing and I was willing to accept my punishment, my father didn't need to bear the brunt too.

I was willing to accept my punishment, but that didn't mean I was feeling good about it and as the adrenaline of the fight wore off, my nerves and feeling of dread grew stronger. The walk seemed to go on forever, which I didn't mind as I was now in no hurry to discover my fate. Eventually we arrived at the guards' building, with the butterflies in my stomach intensifying upon entering.

The superior led me into a small room with nothing but a table and two chairs in the centre of it.

'Take a seat, wait here and keep quiet. Think you can manage that?'

'Yes sir.'

Through a small window in one of the walls, I then watched as the superior entered the adjoining room, sat down behind a large desk and picked up the telephone.

Yes, telephones were back in use to an extent. Not mobiles being carried by everyone and anyone, just the older style ones that were permitted for work related purposes. The superior then spent the next thirty minutes or so involved in a long conversation with someone, and guessing by the looks I was receiving during the call there was no prizes for guessing who the topic of conversation was. The call finally ended and the superior got up from his desk and left the room.

For the next four hours I sat alone and in silence with nothing to do but watch the small clock above the window tick slowly by and fret over my impending punishment.

Just as my eyes began to glaze over and my head bobbed up and down, as I tried to stay awake, finally the door of the room burst open and a rather large imposing figure walked in. From his uniform and battle scarred face, I knew instantly what department he served the Gods in. Why he was here to see me, I had no idea.

'From what I'm hearing, you could be in line for some very serious punishment,' said the man.

'Yes sir, sorry sir.'

He stood over the table, staring down at me in silence for what seemed like an age.

'Your superior, for some unknown reason, has very kindly asked that I take a look at you instead.'

I kept my head down and mouth shut, trying to be as respectful as I could, but my mind was racing with questions.

'Do you know what I do boy?'

'Armed forces, I think sir.'

'Particularly, what I do within the armed forces?'

'No sir.'

'Well boy, the particular area I oversee within the armed forces is the gladiator school. And your superior has been putting forward a very strong argument as to why I should give you a chance to earn a place within my esteemed division.'

I couldn't quite believe what I was hearing and could hold my head down no longer. I looked up at the guard. The move didn't go unnoticed.

'Tweaked your interest now I see,' he commented with a wry smile.

'If I'm honest, had it been anyone other than your superior that had called, I'd have told them not to waste my time. However, I've known your superior a long time and know what type of man he is. He reckons you have talent, raw for sure but adamant as to your potential, given the proper training.

So, let me get to the point. Do you wish to transfer into the armed forces and let us put you to the test or do you wish to remain in this filthy shithole?'

I could only look at the guard, mouth open in shock. Was this really happening?

'I don't have all day boy, yes or no?'

'Yes sir. Definitely yes sir and thank you sir,' I replied, finally finding my voice.

'Alright it's settled then, but let me just give you a little word of warning. I'm not doing you a favour, I'm doing the superior a favour. It's him you owe big style. From what I've heard regarding your behaviour here today, I sense you may be trouble. For the record, I don't like trouble makers and I most certainly don't tolerate them. Understood?'

'Yes sir.'

'If I hear you've caused the slightest bit of bother, you'll be sent back immediately with a swift kick up the arse. And by kick up the arse, I mean a hiding so bad you'll be lucky if you ever walk again. You get me boy?'

'I do, yes sir.'

'Well, we'll find out soon enough. The superior wants a quick word before you go. Once he's done I'll be waiting out front for you.'

'Yes sir,' I replied as the guard left the room and the superior entered a moment later grinning.

'Like the General?' he asked.

'General?'

'Didn't you realise? You've been in lofty company today.'

'No sir I didn't realise and thank you sir. I was expecting.........'

'Punishment?'

'Yes sir.'

'Well, that's exactly what you should be receiving. However, what I witnessed you doing to that crew was no ordinary feat, particularly from a boy of your young age. Trust me, I know a fighter when I see one.'

The superior then lifted his sleeve to reveal a tattoo on his left shoulder. 'You know what that means?'

'Yes sir, everyone knows what that means.' It was a tattoo of a bloodied human skull with a sword protruding out of the top of it. A well-known symbol, worn only by an elite crowd. Gladiators. Winning ones at that. You didn't earn this tattoo just by completing training. No, this symbol was earned with blood in the arena. Only after you had fought and won your first battle, was a gladiator allowed to don this elite symbol.

'You were a gladiator sir?'

'I was, a long time ago now but I still recognise a fellow fighter when I see one and you son, are definitely that. You've a lot to learn but the instinct is there. I know fully trained fighters that couldn't have done what you did to that crew and you're still only fourteen.

Go to the forces, keep your head down, train hard and hopefully you'll love it as much as I did.'

'What happened……..how did…………'

'How did I end up in this shithole?' the superior said what I was trying to find the right words to ask. 'Injury boy. A shitty little injury ended my dream and left me rotting away here. I was good too, could've made champion I reckon, but I got cocky and switched off, too busy entertaining the crowd than paying attention to my opponent. He got the drop on me and managed to injure me before I despatched of him. The recovery took too long and eventually I was deemed too old and unfit to continue as a gladiator, which is a laugh as I could still lace the boots of any of these modern day pussies. Anyway, I was released with honour and made a superior here instead. Once my injury finally healed properly I tried to transfer back several times, but once they're done with you, that's it I'm afraid, there's no way back.

So heed the lesson boy. Even if you reach the top, don't ever let your guard down.'

'Yes sir.'

The superior began laughing to himself. 'I must be going soft with age. Right beat it kid, the General's waiting for you.'

'Yes sir,' I yelled, getting to my feet and heading quick smart for the door. Upon reaching it however, I turned to face the superior once again.

'And thank you sir.'

Chapter 11

As soon as I stepped into the General's vehicle, he took off at breakneck speed across the building site until we arrived at the area my father was working in. Word must have been sent ahead as he was already waiting for us by the roadside, with a guard beside him.

The guard saluted when he realised it was a lofty general and I'm not sure whether he or my dad looked the more nervous.

My Dad climbed into the back seat with me and gave me a look as if to say 'What on earth's going on?' the General turned around to face us both.

'In the most unusual of circumstances, I'm here to inform you that your son has been chosen to transfer into the ranks of the armed forces.'

'Okay,' replied my father sounding confused.

'I'll explain everything in more detail to you and your wife once we arrive at your house. Save me having to explain myself twice,' said the General, clearly feeling rather inconvenienced by the whole affair.

'Yes sir, I understand.'

The tyres then kicked up dirt and sand as the General sped off towards our house.

On arrival, my mother almost broke down on seeing a General's car pull up. This was not a common occurrence and her first thought was something terrible had happened. Her relief at seeing us both alive was short lived, when she heard the news that I was to be transferred to the armed forces. As the General began to explain the events of the day, I was sent to my room to pack for my new life. The armed forces was not a come home every day service like the builders, at least not during training. I would live and breathe the armed forces day and night from my new home, which would be in the very basic form of the recruits' barracks.

I packed away the few belongings I had and was permitted to take, to the noise of my mum sobbing in the living room. The General left the house to wait for me in his car just before my dad opened my bedroom door.

He stood in the centre of the room in silence for a moment, gazing at me with a large grin on his face. 'Well done son, I'm so proud of you,' he finally announced before embracing me with a big bear hug.

'From what I hear, you really gave the crew what for and then some.'

'Thanks Dad.'

The sound of mum crying in the living room, took away his grin for a minute.

'Don't worry about your mother, she knows deep down this is a good thing, but a mother will always worry over her family. The armed forces may be dangerous, but what isn't in the shithole of a world we live in now. At least you can make something of yourself in the armed forces, something to be proud of, not like the builders or any other crappy faction. You've seen it for yourself, so you know what it's like. That will hold you in good stead as all the other recruits in the forces won't have your experience. They won't have your hunger or pain. Use it to make yourself a champion son, be the best. I know it's in you and after today, so should you.'

The General's horn honked impatiently outside.

I hugged my father then went to console my upset mother. She continued to cry as she told me how much she loved me and made me promise to stay alive. I eventually shed a tear or two myself that day but it would be the last time I'd ever cry again.

The General's impatient honking continued outside and my dad urged me to go before he took off without me. With one last hug and goodbye, I set off for my new life in the armed forces.

Chapter 12

It took three hours to drive to the armed forces' training camp that I would be calling home for the next couple of years at least. We sat in silence for the whole journey, which was fine with me as I'd never been further than the building site in all my fourteen years and found the changing landscape extremely interesting, albeit sad at times when we'd drive by large towns or cities that had been obliterated during the landing day attacks.

When we eventually arrived at the training camp and the General stopped the vehicle outside my barracks, he turned around in his seat and stared at me for a long time as if pondering over whether he had made the right choice that day or not.

When he finally turned away and started the engine once more, all he said was, 'Remember my warning boy, I'll be watching closely. Now get out, the Captain will take you from here.'

I was barely out the door with my half-filled backpack before the tyres were screeching away again.

'Follow me boy!' screamed the Captain who had been standing nearby.

I was almost running trying to keep up with the furious march of the Captain as he led me to a building where I filled out some paperwork, collected my uniforms and received my welcome talk.

'You are no longer a person. Your sole purpose is to serve your God Cranock. He demands Victory and Honour above all else. Anything less will be viewed upon as shaming your God. Bring shame upon your God and it will be the last thing you do. Understand?'

'Yes sir.'

'You no longer have a name. Recruits have numbers, and yours will be 686. If you are heard using your old name you will be punished. Understand?'

Yes sir.'

'What's your name boy?'

'686 sir.'

'Right 686, follow me.'

'Yes sir.'

The captain then proceeded to march me around the training complex in a kind of guided tour of the facility. All the time instilling in me the price of failure, laziness, misbehaviour and everything else under the sun. I just continued to nod and say 'Yes sir.' I wasn't going to be found guilty of any of these things, not a chance. I was here to excel and succeed and I planned on doing exactly that.

The Captain finished the tour in the canteen area despite it being well past the dinner meal time. However, a tray had been left aside for me and the Captain instructed I had five minutes to eat as much as I could.

'The food's shit boy, but if you don't eat, you won't have the energy to keep up with the pace here,' he said, which made me chuckle to myself as I was having no problem eating it at all. If he thought this was shit, he obviously hadn't spent much time elsewhere.

This was a treat. Perhaps the rumours of the armed forces being looked after more than any other sector were true.

Full tray demolished with two minutes to spare.

Early in the evening now, the Captain marched me to my final destination. The barracks, where fifty nine other recruits were no doubt awaiting my arrival.

Approaching the doors, a noisy rabble could be heard from within, but as soon as the Captain opened the door, silence fell over the room as everyone immediately stopped what they were doing and stood to attention.

'354'

'Yes sir.'

'Show 686 here to his bunk and get him up to speed with daily routines. Any issues, you'll all be held accountable. Understood?'

'Yes sir,' yelled every single recruit at the top of their lungs.

With that, the captain spun on his heels and left the barracks.

'It's down here,' said 354.

Walking down the middle of the dormitory, I could feel the eyes of every recruit on me. It wasn't unexpected, but uncomfortable all the same.

354 pointed me towards a bottom bunk about three quarters down the right-hand side. Two chests lay at the bottom of the bunks and I emptied my meagre belongings into one of them before lying down on top of my bed. 'What a day,' I thought to myself, before it all caught up with me and I fell into a deep sleep within minutes of lying down.

The loud banging and whistling noise woke me with a start. As I sat up disorientated, the lights were on and all the recruits were scrambling to get into their training gear.

'Get up 686 and get your gear on or we'll all be in the shit,' said a boy from the bunk next to me.

'Oh okay. What are we getting ready to do?' I asked.

'Running. Ten miles through the hills is the most common night time run.'

'Night time run? What time is it?'

'Three am.'

Two instructors were busy pacing up and down the room, screaming at everyone to get a move on, which I duly did and felt good that I at least wasn't the last one to leave the barracks, despite it being my first night and not having a clue as to what was happening.

The run got underway at a brisk pace and as the boy had said, the route was over nearby hills and cross-country terrain. The rude awakening aside, I found the run was like a breath of fresh air to me in more ways than one. My cardio fitness wasn't at the same level as the others, yet I kept pace well enough and still had plenty energy left in the tank by the time we returned to the barracks.

After being dismissed, we trudged back into the dorms to hit the showers and bed again. During the run I had sized up most of the squad and was pleased to discover that I was amongst the tallest and by far one of the strongest looking boys. The years on the building sites had certainly helped my muscles grow at a faster rate than most by the looks of it. Despite this, I found there's always at least one who wants to test you out.

The long drive to the camp earlier in the day had given me plenty time to think about what might lie ahead and I had come to the conclusion that my unusual introduction to a squad that were already two years into their training, might ruffle a few feathers. I envisaged there might be one or two who would want to try and show me who was boss, so to speak. If they did, I promised myself I would make them regret it instantly. A new me was born that day and no one would ever push me around again.

567, as I found out later was his number, probably did me a favour as I emerged from the shower room that night. Heading back to my bunk, 567, who was one of the larger boys and had that bully look written all over his face, walked right into me.

'Thanks for getting us a midnight run bitch.'

I burst out laughing. The fool couldn't have picked a worse person to try and bully at that exact time.

Two scrawny looking boys that appeared to be his henchmen, stood either side of 567, trying their best to look menacing as several other boys quickly gathered round to watch out of interest.

My laughing seemed to have thrown 567 off a little as he looked at me strangely. His face then contorted as he was about to rain some other lame insult towards me. However, before he even had the chance, I closed the space between us in a flash and landed a right hook clean off his jaw.

The blow broke several teeth and sent him sprawling to the ground, barely conscious. His henchmen looked at their downed leader then back at me, with their menacing looks now replaced with fear.

'Pick him up and beat it,' was all I said before sauntering off to my bunk.

'Well done,' said the boy in the bunk next to me with an approving nod. 'He's a prick that's been asking for that since the day we started.'

I lay on my bed with a large grin and thought, 'Job done. Bring on the training!'

Chapter 13

It felt like we were barely back in bed before we were back up for training to begin at 6am. The days were long and hard, with instructors barking orders at you from start to finish, but I loved every minute of it. It was either for you or it wasn't and I could quickly tell whose heart wasn't fully in it. Perhaps if they'd had a taste of life in one of the other sectors first, they'd feel differently.

Most days consisted of running, lots of it, at various times throughout the day and night. As it turns out, the run at 3am the previous night was a common occurrence and nothing to do with my arrival, so the bully 567 was unsurprisingly full of shit. The day was also filled with lots of hand to hand combat and weapons training, particularly swordsmanship, but also including pretty much every other non-gun related weapon you could possibly imagine. Self-defence techniques, mixed martial arts, boxing and anything that could help you develop into a better fighter was taught. This was supposed to be training for every department of the armed forces, but you could see it was definitely tailored towards developing individual fighters, as opposed to an army working together.

They were training us to find the best of the best. The world didn't need armies as it had done before. Sure, the Gods played out battles for their pleasure, but the biggest show and form of entertainment was the gladiator battles. Champion Gladiators won bragging rights for their God. A champion that could entertain and honour his God with victory was what they were all seeking and made no effort to disguise it.

Once basic training had finished at the age of sixteen, if you hadn't already been selected to move into the gladiator specific training camp, then it was unlikely you would. That was the only thing on my mind and the only place I wanted to go.

My strength was well above the average recruit and my cardio was getting stronger by the day. Within the first week I had improved from keeping up to leading the pack. The only area I was behind in was with the weaponry and fighting skills. The other recruits had two years practice on me and it showed. My superior strength helped equal the balance with much of the unarmed combat, however, my sword handling required help and fast.

I spent time in the evening when others were resting to work on the weaponry side of things. The boy in the bunk next to me, no: 231 helped me get up to speed after we became sparring buddies.

Gym work was the only thing not on the training schedule. The camp had an excellent large gym available to use, but it was left for the recruits to decide whether they wanted to give up some of their relatively short rest time in the evening to use it. I think it was actually quite a clever ploy by the instructors, because after a long, hard day of training, not many recruits even considered going to lift some heavy weights. Too tired already and with the thought of another run during the night, most chose to return to the barracks for some down time.

Not me, I wanted to enhance the large muscly frame I had built for myself and keep the strength edge I had over the other recruits. We might be training buddies now, but it wasn't lost on me that one day we could face each other in the arenas. No matter how small or trivial it appeared now, any edge and advantage you might gain over your opponent could be the deciding factor in the end.

The ploy I referred to was also a way for the instructors to see who wanted it most. Who was willing to make the sacrifices in order to become the best of the best. The gym was open to the whole camp, so it wasn't just a few boys from our barracks that would be there, but others from every barrack in the camp. Usually just a handful from each, but even back then you could see the difference. It was the elite from each barrack, the few willing to go the extra mile.

We all knew it too, and there was a kind of grudging respect between us all. However, we also knew we would probably be meeting each other in the annual barrack battles, so there was not much chatting or bonding between us. It was all business, sizing each other up, trying to spot any weaknesses that could be exploited in possible future meetings.

And of course the instructors kept a close eye on things, taking notes on each of us. Even the grumpy General appeared to be sticking to his word of keeping a close eye on me. He kept to the background, but I would always spot him. At first I figured it was him ensuring I wasn't going to be trouble, but as time passed by and his appearances became more frequent, I'm sure it had grown beyond that. I like to think he had become quietly impressed with my progression. By now I was top of my squad by a mile, even excelling in swordsmanship and weaponry handling.

When the annual battle of the barracks arrived, I was selected to represent my barrack in the individual gladiator battles.

Despite being fought with wooden swords and shields, they were taken extremely serious. You could still do some real damage with a wooden sword and many went out their way to do so, with the thinking that if they could badly injure their opponent just now, it would remove a possible candidate from the gladiator training camp and enhance their own chances in the process.

That wasn't my style however, I wanted to make the camp on my own merit, not because another boy had fallen out due to injury. I fought hard but fair. I hurt my opponents but not to a degree that wiped them out of the program. That said, if my opponent tried to play dirty or hobble me, I most definitely let them know how I felt about it and they never tried it again.

I won all my matches in the barracks' battle to become the overall winner, beating most of the boys whose faces I recognised from the nightly gym sessions.

My barrack was given a rare day off from training as an award for my victory, but instead of joining the rest of the barrack lazing about enjoying the extra down time, I continued to train on my own.

I didn't need time off and anyone to enjoy it with. My path was clear to me and training was my pleasure.

As I was busy practising my swordsmanship skills, a voice interrupted me.

'Not enjoying the time off awarded to your barracks? It was you that won it for them after all?'

It was the first time the General had spoken to me since the day he brought me here.

'I enjoy training sir. I'd rather be here working hard, than sitting around the barracks doing nothing.'

The General smiled, which was a first.

'Yes you do, boy. I've been keeping tabs on you and I'm a very hard man to impress, yet you've managed to do just that. My old friend always did have a good eye for talent. He was quite the fighter himself back in the day, did you know that?'

'Yes sir, he showed me his mark.'

'Perhaps one day you'll have the opportunity to earn your own mark.'

'I hope so sir.'

'If you do, let your old superior be a lesson to you. There's no second chances in this game, take your eye off the ball for just a second and your career may be over, possibly your life.'

'Yes sir, I won't sir.'

'We'll see. Anyway, I believe tomorrow holds some significance for you?'

'My fifteenth birthday sir.'

'Well, I have an early gift for you. I'm promoting you into the gladiator camp.'

The unexpected news was easily one of the best, if not *the* best moment of my life, to date. I nearly hugged the General, such was my delight at making the gladiator programme. Becoming a gladiator had become my sole purpose in life and now I was one major step closer to achieving that dream.

'Thank you sir,' I replied, grinning from ear to ear.

'You've earned it boy. You excelled beyond all expectations in basic training and keeping you here would only be holding you back now. You have talent for sure.

A small word of warning before you get ahead of yourself however. Where you're going now is a big step up in class from this. You'll be in with the big boys, the cream of the crop. If you falter or let your standards drop, you'll be pulled from the programme as quickly as you entered it. Understand?'

'Yes sir.'

'Very well, pack your stuff tonight, that's you finished with basic training as of right now. Report to HQ main office at seven am sharp tomorrow, where someone will escort you to your new camp.'

'Yes sir.'

'Well done boy, keep up the standard you've set so far. I'll be watching!'

'Yes sir, thank you sir,' I replied before the General began marching away.

Chapter 14

The next morning I was sat outside the HQ main office with my holdall at 6:30am, eager to get started. Forty five slow minutes later an instructor from the gladiator programme walked through the front doors and marched over to me.

'So, you're the new hot shit then?' he said.

'Erm.......Yes sir,' I replied unsure how to answer that without sounding big headed or cocky.

He smirked then said, 'We'll see. Get your stuff then and follow me.'

We left the HQ building and drove to the area designated for the gladiator programme. It was still within the whole armed forces training camp but quite a distance from where I had been doing my basic training and it was another eye opener to see just how vast the area assigned to the armed forces was.

When we passed through the entrance gates of the gladiator training camp, you could see the difference from the basic training camp immediately. The buildings, the facilities, weapons and more importantly, the recruits all looked a huge step up from where I had just come from.

Watching the various groups training as we drove through the camp, you could see the difference in size, fitness and skill of what you would need to call men now, as opposed to the boys in basic training.

The clashes of metal against metal rang out loud as some of the young men practised with real swords instead of wooden ones.

We passed by an actual gladiator arena, much smaller than the ones used for the main events, but big enough to impress a passing fifteen year old boy. When we finally stopped outside the main office facility, I had to admit to feeling a little overawed.

Inside I swapped one uniform for another, with the new one proudly identifying me as part of the gladiator programme. I was given directions to my accommodation and told to rendezvous with my new squad in one hour.

My accommodation turned out to be a two storey building, comprising of fifty separate rooms. No more sharing a dorm with ninety nine other boys. I now had a room all to myself that even had its own bathroom. This was luxury as far as I was concerned.

I emptied my bag and changed into my training gear before setting off to meet my new squad and instructor, whose first act was to shout the do's and don'ts for the gladiator training camp at me in front of the whole squad, whilst they all eyeballed the latest recruit, sizing me up. I can't blame them, I was doing the exact same thing as I cast my gaze over the whole squad, one by one. Well developed for my age, together with the hard training regime I impressed on myself, I found that I was still one of the tallest, fittest and strongest looking among the squad, despite some of them nearing the end of the programme as they approached their eighteenth birthday. If you hadn't made the grade by then, it was all over and your future career lay elsewhere, which I soon found out made some of the older recruits particularly sneaky and vicious. Bitter at the realisation it probably wasn't going to happen for them, they lashed out their frustrations by trying to end some of the younger recruits' careers.

Rather than weed out this behaviour however, the instructors almost encouraged it, viewing it as just another aspect of training that would help you improve as a fighter. Not sure I agreed with the morals of that one, but that's just the way it was.

It was the same in basic training, just the stakes and dangers were much higher at this level. People didn't just get injured in gladiator camp, many suffered the ultimate fate, death.

From there the training took off hard and fast. It was indeed a huge step up from basic training, but I thrived on it.

Much in the same way as I had done in basic, I learned, adjusted, then excelled. By the time my sixteenth birthday was just under a month away, I had risen to become the leader of my squad again.

There wasn't much in the way of bonding and friendships in the gladiator camp and that suited me just fine. I preferred to train and learn without any distractions, however, on the rare occasions the squad got talking, the chat would usually revolve around killing. Some eager to know what it's like to take a life or more truthfully, probably wondering whether they had it in them. Some would try to act macho and boast about how they'd do it and then there was the odd few that had already killed within the training regime. They usually kept out of the conversation, their talking had already been done for them by their actions.

I think it would be fair to assume the topic of 'your first kill' had run through the head of pretty much every single recruit that had joined the armed forces. My aim from day one had always been to join the gladiator ranks and therefore I had many a daydream of fighting in a packed arena, winning obviously and therefore killing in the process. At that point in time I had no idea just how cut-throat the gladiator camp would be.

The longer I was in the regime and witnessed how deadly the training alone could be, you start to imagine that there's a strong possibility your first kill could come much sooner than the glory of the arena.

And so, when that turned out to be the case for me, it came as no real shock and I found I gave it little afterthought. That may sound cold, however, we were in the game of death. We all knew and accepted the risks willingly. You might have been drafted into the armed forces without a choice, but no one entered the gladiator programme that didn't want to be there.

Another reason why I might not have cared too much over the boy I killed, was the fact that he was one of the older, spiteful recruits who was on his way out of the programme.

During a one on one battle to submission, he swung at my neck well after the instructor had told us to break. When we commenced again I took him down quickly and aggressively. My sword entered deep into his stomach. As he lay on the ground groaning, I glanced towards the instructor to ensure I wasn't in trouble. Far from it, the instructor spoke loudly to ensure the other recruits stopped to watch, albeit most of them were already doing so with the noise of the wounded boy groaning on the floor.

'He went for you after the break 686, and tried to kill you. If it was me, I'd kill him. However, the choice is yours. Finish it or let him go to the infirmary!'

My mind was made instantly and I sank my sword down into the boy's heart without hesitation. If I wanted to become a gladiator, that was the only choice to make and the instructors knew it too. Had I let him live, my days in the programme would have been over. A gladiator that doesn't have the stomach for killing is never going to grace the arenas.

As the boy's body was dragged away, I went for lunch with the rest of the squad. I expected my first kill to be more of an event and something that might have played on my mind for a little while at least, but it never did. Not in the slightest.

So that was my first kill. It definitely wasn't going to be my last.

Chapter 15

Looking back, I believe I was partnered with that boy by the instructors intentionally, hoping for that very situation to play out to enable them to put my killer instinct to the test.

For only one week later, I was instructed to report to the General's office.

'Your progress has continued to flourish I'm pleased to say. Your instructors believe you are one of the finest recruits they've trained,' said the General as he rose from behind his desk and slowly paced around the room, and me, as I stood to attention in the centre of his office.

'Thank you sir,' I replied.

'Your fitness is remarkable, as is your growth and development. Your body is already adult like and remind me again, what height are you now?'

'Six foot five sir.'

'Any concerns after taking your first life last week?'

'No sir.'

'Problems sleeping? Guilty conscious? Apprehension?'

'No sir, none at all.'

'Good to hear. Happy to kill again then?'

Yes sir. Eager to do so sir.'

The General raised an eyebrow at me.

'In the arena sir. Eager to fight and kill in the arena.'

The General bore a wry smile as he nodded his head.

'Well 686, I'm going to put that eagerness to the test right now. Our God is very much a believer in if you're good enough, you're old enough, as am I. He expects us to keep his gladiator contests engaging and interesting spectacles. Develop champions that the crowd will adore. Which isn't as easy as you'd think.

We've had gladiators make their debuts at a young age before, however, none have graced a full, main arena contest at the tender age of sixteen. I want you to be the first.'

'Of course sir, I'd be honoured.'

'Fantastic boy. This could be the start of something special for you. Everyone takes to a young fighter, the women cry, picturing their own young sons, and the men admire the bravery of gracing the arena at such an early age. They'll be on your side before the battle even begins. Once it does, put on a spectacle that I know you're capable of doing and they won't forget you. Do that and you'll have gained a following in one fight that others may not get until they have won at least five or six battles. Your birthday is in three weeks. I've suggested we have the battle on the day of your birthday. What better way to celebrate?'

'Yes sir, indeed,' I replied, a little in shock that my dream of becoming a gladiator was actually about to come true, and much earlier than anyone could have imagined.

'I'll make sure your parents get priority tickets and even allow you to spend some time with them after the show, all going well obviously.'

'Yes sir, thank you sir,' I said wondering how my mother would take the news that her son was about to fight a gladiator battle on his sixteenth birthday. Not well I predicted.

'Very well 686, return to your training and keep doing what you do best. Don't let this news distract your focus.'

'I won't sir.'

'And keep it to yourself for now boy. I'll let you know once the arrangements have been finalised and then we'll start prepping you.'

'Yes sir and thank you again sir.'

'Just don't let me down.'

'I won't sir.' Just as I was leaving the General's office he called me back.

'One more thing 686.'

'Yes sir?'

'You'll need a name. Numbers are for recruits. Fully fledged gladiators have names.'

He was correct of course, it just wasn't something I'd given any thought to. Some of the boys had names picked for themselves from the moment they arrived at basic training, but I always felt it was being presumptuous, as most of them never even came close to using them.

'You don't need to give me the name just now, just have it ready for the prep team next week. And choose wisely!'

Yes sir, I will.'

The General then waved me off, signalling the meeting was over.

Chapter 16

Over the course of the following week I continued to train at my normal high intensity, yet it was impossible not to think about my upcoming debut in the arena. I was nervous and excited in equal measures. The hardest thing I had been finding was trying to choose a gladiator title for myself.

I finally settled on the name The Destroyer, albeit it was more out of desperation minutes before I was due to meet the prep team, than a well thought out process.

The prep team turned out to be pretty much solely concerned with the promotion of the fight rather than prepping me for it. That didn't come as a major surprise however, having seen many pre fight broadcasts before. There wasn't much transmitted on the home screens, so when something did go live, most people took notice.

They were generally short and to the point broadcasts, informing the people of dates and times of upcoming gladiator battles and who was fighting who. Clips of the various fighters in action would be shown and interviews held with certain fighters, usually just the champions or popular challengers, never debutants.

That's why it came as a surprise to discover the prep team wanted to do an interview with myself. Apparently, the instruction from above was to make a big deal over my youthful age. I wasn't keen on the idea at all but I didn't really have a choice in the matter.

I cringe when I think about the interview now. I was more nervous doing that interview than I had ever been in my life and it felt so awkward being sat down in front of a strange machine and asked questions that I would generally never have discussed with anyone. I hated it, it was horrible and it showed. I feared I would find myself in trouble for such an incompetent performance. Strangely, my superiors loved it. Apparently it was exactly what they were hoping for, feeling it would suck everyone in to thinking I was a sad unfortunate fifteen year old boy way out of his depth. When in actual fact they knew on the battle ground where it counted, I was anything but. The prep team were instructed to not show any clips of me in training in order to keep up the pretence of me being a lamb being put to the slaughter.

To give them their dues, it worked really well. I was later informed that I had become probably the most talked about debutant in the history of the games, albeit most conversations were predicting how I would die or be slaughtered, but still, just as the General had predicted, I had grown a following before even setting foot in the arena.

Chapter 17

My sixteenth birthday, the day of the fight eventually arrived. I reported to the main office building just before 7am and was surprised to find that the General himself would be transporting me to the arena. We took off at his usual break neck speed and around an hour later found ourselves at the mighty colosseum.

It was a jaw dropping sight and could be seen towering above the ground for miles around. I'd seen it many times on previous broadcasts, but this was the first time in person. The fights weren't due to begin until late afternoon but the General had deliberately arrived early to enable me to explore the arena and get the feel of the place, to avoid being overawed by the occasion.

Easier said than done, as we took a walk onto the sand and I looked around at the towering rows upon rows of spectator galleries overlooking the battleground. It was exciting and intimidating and it was still empty at that point. I tried to imagine what it would be like when it was full.

We spent the rest of the day in the lower levels of the colosseum, where there were several large gym areas for the fighters to warm up and practise. Opposing fighters were kept apart until the actual contest so you were assigned which gym and other facilities you would be permitted to use.

Unlike the cut-throat atmosphere of the training schools, there was a great deal of respect between the other fighters I encountered, with many of them wishing me luck.

As the day wore on, the noise from the arena above me grew and grew to the point I was sure the ceiling was going collapse on top of me, as the crowd stamped and cheered and celebrated the first contest of the day.

Another unusual honour I had received was the position of my contest. Most debutants would be the first fight of the day, with the biggest contest, usually featuring the current champion, being the last. However, my age had caused such a stir and interest, my fight had been moved up to the middle stages of the show.

It was an exciting day but also one of the longest as I waited with growing butterflies in my stomach for my fight to finally arrive. Hence, my overwhelming feeling was relief when I was eventually instructed to gather my weapons and make my way to the arena entrance.

Some contests the weapons would be chosen for you and others you were allowed to pick your own. Being my debut, I was given the choice and two swords were my preferred option.

The General accompanied me as far as he was allowed to, then with a wry smile said, 'Don't let me down kid.'

'I won't sir.'

'Go through the door and follow the tunnel until you reach another member of staff. They'll instruct you when to enter the arena from there. Good luck,' said the arena staff escorting us, who were basically armed forces drafted in for the events. I entered the door inscribed 'Gladiators Only' and began walking through the long tunnel, alone with my thoughts and the noise of the arena above me.

Reaching the end of the tunnel, as expected another guard wished me good luck and informed me that on his signal, the door before us would rise and I would enter the arena.

As we stood in silence for a few minutes, I listened to the arena announcer introduce my opponent, which seemed to bring a mixed response from the crowd.

The staff member then looked at mc and said, 'Here goes, thrcc, two, one!'

The door in front of us shot up suddenly, allowing heat and light to burst into the tunnel. The noise level increased another few decibels however, it was nothing compared to when I stepped out onto the sand. The noise went through the roof as I began walking towards the centre of the arena. I paused to look around and marvel at the now full galleries. It truly was a sight to behold and despite making many more appearances at the colosseum, that first experience of walking onto the sand is one that I will take to the grave with me.

As awesome as the arena was, I was here for a reason and quickly told myself to focus. I did my best to block out the surroundings upon reaching the centre of the sand, where my awaiting opponent stood.

We engaged in a staring contest, sizing each other up. He was putting on a brave face but I could see in his eyes he was a little taken aback at my height and physique. The prep team had done a good job of portraying an innocent boy, hiding my height and physique from the camera as best they could and it appeared it wasn't just the audience that had been fooled somewhat.

My opponent had clearly been thinking he was in for an easy night and was now feeling foolish. He had two victories to his name already though, so he couldn't have been without any skill. By the time we had finished sizing each other up, my confidence was rising.

Suddenly the crowd fell silent as Cranock took to his feet to address the arena. As I had been instructed beforehand, my opponent and I sank one knee onto the sand as a show of respect to our God. I had been so taken with everything else going on I almost forgot a God would be watching me fight. The arena was so big and from my view in the centre of it, he was a distant figure to look at, but just to know you were in his presence was a big deal.

When your life is on the line, you shouldn't really need any further motivation to perform but just in case anyone did, knowing a God was watching you should do it, as disappointing them would be an extremely foolish thing to do.

The announcer had already done the necessary pre fight speech, leaving just the signal to begin the contest to Cranock. It was really just a chance for everyone to show respect to their God and for him to remind them all who was the boss. Not that anyone was in need of reminding.

Satisfied he had received his due respect, he motioned for us the fighters to rise to our feet and prepare ourselves for the battle to commence.

At this point you could hear a pin drop in the huge arena, before he finally announced the beginning of the contest with one word,

'FIGHT!'

After his command the silence was immediately replaced with a roar from the crowd unlike anything I'd ever heard in my life. Every time I fought in the colosseum it never failed to send a rush of adrenalin coursing through my body.

My opponent charged forward from the off, probably hoping I would make a slow start after being overawed by the occasion, but he was wrong and only brought about his own death quicker. It could have been quicker yet. He attacked wildly with his sword, causing his defensive shield to move out of position, leaving a gap that I could have thrust my sword straight through into his heart and that would have been it all over. However, the General's advice of putting on a good show for the crowd was still fresh in my memory and therefore I resisted the easy kill and opted for a bit of blood and gore for the watching audience.

I blocked his attack with one sword, then sent my other crashing down upon his wooden shield, splintering the top half on impact. Before he knew what was happening I moved behind him and stamp kicked his back to send him sprawling onto the sand.

A deafening cheer arose from the crowd and I decided to use their support as a ruse for my opponent. I began playing to the crowd, much to their enjoyment. To my opponent it would look like foolish overconfidence. However, as I waved to the crowd, I never once took my eye off him. It may have appeared that way but from the corner of my eye I kept track of his every movement.

He took the bait readily and rushed in for another ill prepared attack. The crowd erupted in noise, believing as he did, that I was not paying attention to what I should be.

I kept up the pretence until the last second, as he rushed forward and thrust his sword towards my back, his face a picture of disbelief at how sloppy I could be. It changed in an instant however, as I suddenly stepped to the side, turning around in the process and bringing one of swords slicing down through his extended arm.

As his arm and sword fell to the ground, I continued to move around my shocked opponent until I stood behind him. His shield arm was being held slightly out from his body and I brought my sword racing upwards through the gap, chopping off his other arm close to the shoulder joint.

He screamed in horror before falling to his knees, glancing to and fro at his bloodied limbs lying on the sand.

I now raised both my swords and held them aloft for a moment as the crowd continued to cheer my performance, then arced my swords around, criss-crossing them as they sliced through my opponent's neck and chopped his head clean off.

And that was it. My first ever gladiator battle, over within a savage couple of minutes. The crowd was going wild, despite realising I wasn't quite the small innocent sixteen year old boy they believed was being thrown to the wolves. I was still sixteen, and for any boy of that age to grace the arena deserved credit.

I waved to the applauding crowd, revelling in the glory, and to this day it is still one of the best feelings I've ever had in my life. Before exiting the sand, as per protocol I bowed to Cranock to show my respect and unbelievably he stood up and applauded me. I was gobsmacked, a God was actually applauding me!

I couldn't stop smiling as I left the arena, my dream had been fulfilled and it had actually been far easier than I could have expected. Harder fights were to come of course but you can only deal with what's in front of you and I had done so explicably well.

That thought was backed further as I entered the changing area to find the General applauding me with a smile as large as my own.

The smile never left my face until I met my parents an hour later and the first thing my mom did was slap me on the face for all the worry and anxiety I had been causing her. I couldn't blame her and she quickly followed it with a giant hug and told me how much she loved and missed me.

You tend to forget it can't be easy for any mother to watch their son taking a man's life in a gruesome manner, not to mention the stress and worry of wondering whether it would be me left in a bloody mess on the sand.

She didn't know whether to laugh or cry, give me a row for taking a life or congratulate me on the victory.

I'd been so consumed with my own goal for the last few years and being surrounded by only other like-minded individuals, it made you forget that not everyone revelled in the blood sport of the gladiators. Also, it was the first time we had seen each other since I left for the armed forces, which brought about emotions of its own.

All in all, seeing the inner struggle of my mother dealing with it, brought my feet back to ground and that was probably a good thing.

My dad was over the moon with me and my performance, going through it excitedly step by step, once out of earshot of my mother.

It was great to see them both again and to hear them say how proud they were of me. I replied likewise and said the only reason I had achieved this much, was down to their efforts as parents. Emotions ran high and more tears flowed when we were forced to say our goodbyes.

When the General drove us back to camp a short while later, I was already looking forward to my next contest in the arena.

Chapter 18

The following morning I was instructed to gather my belongings and report to the main office building to be re-housed. Now a fully-fledged gladiator, I had outgrown the recruits' training programme and was now being promoted in the world.

Fully fledged gladiators, especially the good ones, were among the best treated servants of the Gods. Most were gifted with luxury homes and the champions were often gifted living quarters in the Gods' own great pyramids.

I wasn't quite on that level yet and although I had outgrown the recruits, I hadn't left the overall camp yet. There was an area, off limits to most that served, as a living area for the young, newly fledged gladiators.

The area had top notch training facilities and a canteen where the food had improved yet again. Other more elite gladiators who lived off camp in more luxurious accommodation would still come by to use the facilities and train with the other gladiators.

I was shown to a basic small house, much like the one I had grown up in. The house formed part of a row and there were many rows. Moving my belongings into the house, which didn't need more than two trips to the car, the gladiator from the neighbouring house appeared to welcome me and introduced himself as Cody. After talking for a while, I enquired about the previous tenant for some reason and was informed that I had just killed him. You had to laugh at the irony.

I now trained with other gladiators and soon found, as I had done at the colosseum, the atmosphere was more friendly and respectful. There was no longer the bitterness or fear of not making it, from the training camps. No one was attempting to injure anyone else and I was informed that if anyone did try that, they would most likely be killed by the other gladiators.

Not that they didn't train hard. They most certainly did, and there would always be the odd grudge held or basic dislike of one person or another, but if that was the case then the issue would normally be dealt with inside the arena.

The whole friendship thing was a little strange at first, having spent so long in training where everyone is competing against each other in such a way that you don't really bond as friends. Cody knew how I felt, having entered the gladiator camp himself not so long ago, and was a great help to me in adjusting to a slightly different way of life. We had become friends and it made me sad when he died just three months later during his next fight. I quickly learned that was just the way it went, your neighbours tended to change quickly round these parts.

After Cody died I decided there was no point making good friendships as they would most likely be short lived and any feelings of grief or sadness could just serve to put you off your game. From that point on, I was polite and respectful but avoided starting any friendships and concentrated solely on training and winning. And that I did well.

I fought another five fights, winning well and entertaining the audience in the following year since my first contest. After that, I was rewarded once again with a new home, this time it was off-camp. A bigger, nicer house, complete with a black electric SUV in the driveway. I didn't really need any of it, I was quite happy in my smaller apartment, close to the training facilities, but it wouldn't go down well to throw a gift from a God back in their face, so I moved on graciously. The car was fun I have to admit and despite being a little hesitant at first, I soon began to love tearing around the deserted roads in it as I made the journey to and from my training camp each day. There was also one other major benefit that made the whole move worthwhile. Music!

It was the General who had taken the time out to show me to my new home, not something he'd done personally with other gladiators, and he pointed out that my television screen was a little different to most others. Generally they were like the one we had in my parents' house that would only come on when the Gods wanted something broadcast. There were no functions on it other than that.

My new one, I found could be turned on and used to play libraries worth of music from years well before the Gods' had arrived. The General tried to tell me it was like a new age jukebox but whatever he meant by that was lost on me.

Music was a thing of the past, at least for families like mine, growing up in the lower levels of our new society. I'd never listened to any music or had the means to do so. This was something alien to me, but I absolutely loved it. From the minute I got in from training I would flick through the millions of songs from different decades of our past and listen to the varying styles of music. I found it was a great way to relax and switch off from the non-stop training or thoughts about an up-coming fight.

As I stood waiting beside the door that led onto the sand, for my eighth contest, I suddenly had a great idea.

After my victory, I sought out the General and asked if I could be granted permission to play a song through the arena's PA system as I made my entrance onto the sand. With a wry smile, he said he would run my request up the chain of command and get back to me.

Several weeks later I was informed by the General of my next fight and also that my request had been granted. I set to work trying to choose the right song, which proved to be easier said than done, but eventually I settled on the song – Sad But True, by a heavy metal band called Metallica.

It definitely wasn't the kind of music that would appeal to everyone but as far as music to make a grand entrance into a gory fight to the death goes, it was perfect!

And so, when my ninth fight came around and the doorway to the sand shot open, I motioned to the guard to give the order to play my song.

I remained in the tunnel for a moment and listened as the heavy rock notes burst through the arena and sent the crowd into a shocked silence. Nodding my head in beat with the drums, I finally emerged onto the sand and actually burst out laughing as I looked at all the shocked faces littering the galleries. I had to remind myself that most of them hadn't heard music for decades, if at all. No wonder they were in shock at being blasted with a heavy rock song like this. Upon reaching halfway however, I noticed a change and by the time I reached my opponent, the crowd was now going crazy.

My poor shell-shocked opponent looked disturbed and never recovered in time as I made quick work of him in my now notoriously efficient, gory manner.

After the fight, I was wondering how our God Cranock would have enjoyed the entrance, when I was duly instructed that I would not be permitted any further requests for music being played during my entrance. That answered that question.

Thankfully he couldn't have found my entrance too disrespectful, as I was also informed that I had now earned the right to challenge the reigning champion.

Which more or less brings us up to the present time. One month before my eighteenth birthday, I stand on the cusp of greatness, ready to battle with the current undefeated, longest reigning champion. Victory will see me take his title and become the youngest ever gladiator champion. No simple task however, and easily my toughest opponent yet.

Whilst warming up in my allocated open training area, I hear raised voices before a large, well-built man, bursts through one of the doors and heads in my direction. I quickly realise it's the champion breaking protocol by coming to see me, and judging by the melee of guards following in his wake, he's being told precisely that. However, other than a God himself, who's really going to be able to stop a champion gladiator from going where he wants to?

I'm beginning to wonder if I should be preparing to engage in combat when he raises his hands in a show of peace.

'I'm very sorry sir,' shouts one of the trailing guards. 'We tried to tell him this was against protocol.'

'Its fine, I'm sure he's aware of the protocol, but leave us, no word shall be spoken of any breach of your duties, I promise.'

The guards look doubtful but eventually begin to backtrack.

'Thanks, they're relentless,' laughs the champion.

'You can't blame them, they're just fearful of being reprimanded for failing to do their duties.'

'I know, but as you said, no one's going to be sticking them in it.'

I nod in agreement. 'So, what brings the reigning champion to see me?'

'In thirty-seven contests, I've only come to see two opponents before you. Only two from thirty-seven have I deemed worthy of competing for my title. You're now the third.'

'I'm honoured,' I reply truthfully.

'You've earned it son. I've watched your fights and you're an exceptional talent, probably the best I've faced yet. Although I did say that to the other two and........well........I'm the one standing here. So be warned, I'm not ready to give up the title yet, but I'm also long enough in the tooth to recognise and admire a great gladiator when I see one.'

He then stepped forward and outstretched his hand to shake.

As I accepted the offer and shook his hand, he added, 'Good luck son. Whoever walks out of the arena today will be a worthy champion.'

His honest and gracious words stuck with me and made me respect and admire the man even more than I did already. He was a true champion.

Walking out of my training area he called back with a grin on his face, 'Of course, it'll still be me though.'

A short while later, I stood in the centre of the arena and watched as he made his entrance to the sand and wallowed in the adulation of the crowd. It was the first time I had heard the crowd roar for an opponent of mine as loudly as they had done for myself. It was almost a shame that the world would lose a fine gladiator no matter who won. Such was the nature of our life.

Readying ourselves to commence the battle, gone was any look of respect and friendship in our eyes. Now replaced with a steely determination to win at all costs.

The fight began at a frantic pace as we both tested out each other's skills. I had definitely found a new level altogether and could see why he had been a deserved champion for so long. He too, fought with two swords which landed much heavier than anyone I had faced previously and his reactions were lightning fast too.

The sound of metal clashing against metal rang out as we pushed each other back and forward in a display of skilled swordsmanship worthy of the occasion. The crowd were mesmerised.

The pace was relentless and would have been tiring for some, but my fitness was incredible and allowed me to perform at this level without dropping my concentration for an instant. Perhaps this was the reason that when the first mistake was made, it was by the older opponent.

It was barely even a mistake and would have gone unnoticed against most other fighters, but not me. In a flash I drew first blood and nicked a small gash across the champion's right thigh. A collective gasp arose from the spectators as the fighting broke for a moment, for the first time since the bout began.

Catching our breath, he glanced at his wound then towards me with a wry smile and gave a nod of acknowledgement. Before I could even react, he launched forward with a roar and began another furious attack. It was clever, feigning the injury was affecting him in anyway by emphasising the attack. It wasn't new, many tried to do the same thing, but were unable to do it so well, but I noticed the slight difference in his movement and bided my time until the opening presented itself. When it did, I opened a bigger and slightly nastier gash across his other thigh.

It's great to win fights in glorious big hits like slicing an arm off, however sometimes, particularly against a highly skilled opponent you have to be patient and build up to the glory shots by applying smaller intricate, injuries first. Slowing your opponent and knocking their confidence until they are ready for a grand finish.

The next time we clashed I sliced open his left achilles, which now hampered him so much, even the spectators could see it. His time was over. Not that he was accepting it yet, nor would I expect him to, but if I was to lose the contest now I would only have myself to blame.

He attacked through frustration and anger allowing me to send the tip of my blade deep into his side abdomen. I withdrew the sword and stepped aside as he fell onto his knees and the crowd fell silent, unsure whether to cheer for the soon-to-be new champion or respect the much-loved reigning one's last moments.

I almost felt bad for winning. Almost, but not quite. I circled the champion slowly and glanced towards

Cranock, hoping for some kind of intervention but none came. I stopped in front of the downed champion and watched as he breathed heavily whilst holding his injured abdomen.

'Well done champ,' he said as his eyes rose to meet mine. 'Had to happen eventually, I'm glad it was to someone worthy. Now stop fucking around and finish me!'

Without another word I stepped forward and stabbed my sword into his chest and through his heart. He didn't deserve to have his head chopped off in a show for the audience. I pulled my sword free, then slowly lowered his body onto the sand.

You could have heard a pin drop as I walked away from his body. Upon reaching the centre of the arena I raised one of my swords aloft and the crowd erupted in noise as they celebrated a new King of the Colosseum.

Chapter 19

Three days after becoming the new champion gladiator, I was relaxing in my home when the General arrived unexpectedly. He informed me that I had been invited to the great pyramid to meet our God Cranock, and that I was to bring my belongings with me as I would be shown to my new living quarters within the pyramid itself.

I had grown to really like my current home, with the music and the enjoyable drive to camp each day, but once again what could I say. It wasn't so much of an invite as it was an order, so great pyramid here I come.

And great was an understatement. If I thought the colosseum was jaw dropping when I first approached it, then this was on another level altogether. It was hard to even comprehend the sheer size of it. A huge megacity all within the one structure. It was so high that sometimes you couldn't see the top part of it because of the clouds. On a clear day, which it was most of the time, as a young child I would stare at it from afar in wonder.

The very top part of the structure was Cranock's living quarters and I wondered what the view must be like from up there. It was unlikely I would ever find out as not many humans ever ventured there, apart from a few trusted members of staff, like cooks and cleaners. But they were sworn to silence and would be killed without hesitation if found to be discussing private matters to others.

I made a promise to myself to try and find out one day, but realistically, I knew it was unlikely to happen.

Nearing the foot of the building, the General pressed a button in his car and a large entranceway opened up for us to drive into. We continued through a long tunnel until it opened up into a large room that was littered with rows upon rows of cars. All types, various colours and makes, and without doubt the most cars I'd ever seen in my life.

'It's something eh,' said the General with a smile. He once told me he had been a 'bit of a petrol head' back in the day before the Gods arrived. I wasn't exactly sure what he meant but I'd picked up on the fact he liked his cars and took great joy in being one of the few individuals on the planet that still got to drive one. Having grown up knowing very little about them, I wasn't particularly interested when I had received one with my last home. However, that view changed very quickly once I started tearing around the deserted roads in it and now it was quickly becoming a passion we shared.

That passion reached a new high when the General stopped the car before a row of three super fancy looking vehicles.

'Come on, take a look at these,' he said exiting the vehicle.

The first one was blue with two large white stripes going down the centre of the vehicle and was apparently called a Mustang Shelby GT500. The second was a sleek red car called a Ferrari and the third was a much larger, black vehicle called a Range Rover.

'You like?' asked the General.

'Yeah, they look amazing,' I reply, stating the obvious.

'Well that's good seeing as they're yours,' he said laughing.

'What?'

'They're yours. A gift from Cranock. You can thank him shortly, then perhaps we can take them out for a test drive?'

This time I laughed as I thought the test drive was as much for the General's benefit as it was mine.

'Sounds good to me.'

The General then parked his car in an allocated spot nearby and we began making our way towards an elevator. I'd never set foot in one in my life and made a strange noise as it began climbing the building at furious speed, which made me feel like I had left my stomach on the ground floor. The General seemed to find it all very amusing.

The lift slowed suddenly, making my stomach lurch once again. 'That'll take a bit of getting used to,' I said as the elevator doors opened.

We then made our way down a large corridor until we arrived at a door with the number 686 on the front of it. I raised an eyebrow and looked at the General.

'I'm guessing that's not a coincidence?'

'Just a little something to remind you where you came from and hopefully prevent that head of yours getting any bigger.'

I knew he meant well and was part joking, part telling the truth, and he was probably right. It was no easy feat becoming a gladiator, never mind a champion one, but if you managed it the rewards were great. Greater than any other human could ever hope to achieve and it was no secret that the Gods held their prized fighters in the highest regard and rewarded them well. Sometimes it was easy to forget just how hard and how much of a struggle day to day life was for most of the population on the New Earth. But then most of the population didn't put their life on the line as I did.

High risk, high reward was apparently a very old saying that was still very true to this day.

I placed my hand on a small scanning device and the door opened up to reveal my new luxurious living quarters. The apartment, if you could call it that was huge and split over three levels, with the lower level comprising of a fully equipped gym, training area, sauna and steam room.

The top level was the sleeping area and my bed was the most ridiculous thing I'd ever seen. It was huge and left me thinking I'd feel lost in it, having slept in small, basic single beds for most of my life. The bathroom, just off the bedroom, which the General informed me was called an en-suite, was bigger than most folk's houses.

There was a walk in bath that blew bubbles around to relax you if you pressed a certain button, another small steam room and shower that could probably fit ten adults under it at the same time.

And then of course there was the living area on the entrance level. It wasn't so much what was on the inside of this area than the view of the outside. Thick glass ran the length of the living area, offering the most spectacular view over the land as far as the eye could see. It was yet another jaw dropping view on a day that seemed full of them.

'Has it got music?' I ask, motioning towards a gigantic television screen that adorned one of the interior walls.

'It's got more than that. Check it out,' replies the General. 'Films on screen,' he adds and the screen bursts into life, listing off different genres.

'Films?'

'Yep. Pretty much every film that was ever made is now available to you 24/7.'

'Wow,' I was blown away. I'd never seen a single film in my whole life but had heard plenty about them from my parents and other older folk. I couldn't wait to get started on watching some of them for real.

'You should check out the games too. Believe me, they'll blow your mind. For now however, we need to head upstairs to meet you know who and you definitely don't want to be late for that.

As we left my deluxe new apartment, the General said, 'One more thing. Whatever you do just make sure you keep the noise down.'

'Okay sir, does Cranock not like any loud noise?'

'No stupid, *I don't*! And I live down there,' he said jokingly, pointing towards another door further down the corridor.

The General led us to another elevator, different from the first one and we climbed higher still in the great pyramid. We exited the elevator and entered a reception type area with a lady sitting behind a large desk and two armed guards standing either side of it.

The guards immediately saluted the General before the lady said rather curtly, 'Please take a seat for now, someone will come and escort you shortly.'

Soon enough another pair of guards appeared to escort us and a short walk later, we were led into a large room, lined with many weird and wonderful artefacts.

A moment or two later, a set of double doors opened and the imposing figure of Cranock marched into the room. The two guards and the General immediately dropped to one knee and I quickly followed suit.

'Rise,' commanded the God, before instructing the two guards to leave.

He was a tall and imposing figure, but so was I and as he stood before me, I reckoned I was just slightly taller.

'Congratulations young champion. You've proved yourself to be a very talented gladiator.'

'Thank you, my lord,' I reply.

'You fight with skill and above all, a zest for victory. Embellishing the two morals I hold above all else, honour and victory. I do not accept defeat and I see that same feeling burning within you. For these combined reasons, I have chosen you to lead my army into a battle against the Goddess Petra's army.'

'Thank you, my lord, it will be an honour.'

Cranock moved closer and stared at me for a moment with his piercing eyes, before continuing with a raised voice.

'It is indeed an honour and the highest any human can perform for his God. I am trusting you to lead my army to victory and anything other than that will bring shame and embarrassment upon me. That will not be tolerated, do you understand me, gladiator?'

'I do, my lord. I will bring you victory.'

'From what I've seen, I'm sure you will,' he said, lowering his voice again. 'Serve your God well and you will be rewarded as I'm sure you're already well aware of. Do you like the gifts I have granted you for your success so far?'

'I do very much and I am very thankful for them, my lord.'

'Then continue to serve me well with further victories and the gifts will continue to fall at your feet.'

'I will, my lord.'

'Now to business then. Each army will be allowed five thousand men. As leader of my army, it will be your responsibility to pick and train the fighters. A broadcast will go out to the world soon announcing the battle, which will commence in three months' time. Anything you need, speak to the General here and it will be arranged. Understood?'

'Yes, my lord.'

'Very well, good luck young gladiator. I look forward to seeing you in three months.'

As Cranock turned and began walking away, the General and I dropped to one knee again until he had left the room, at which point the two guards re-appeared and began escorting us back to the elevator.

We remained silent until the doors closed over and it was just the two of us. The General then looked at me with his wry smile and said, 'That's a big one kid. Beat another God's army for Cranock and you'll be moving right up to the top with him.'

He was right of course. Perhaps not about me moving up to the top of the great pyramid, but the battles between God's armies were the only thing bigger than the gladiator contests.

'Do I really get to choose the entire army, without interference?' I ask the general upon reaching the corridor of our apartments.

'Yeah, you sure do.'

'Anyone at all?'

'Am I not speaking English? Yes, anyone at all, the choice is all yours. Now go and enjoy the trapping of your success for the rest of the day, then first thing, we'll take two of your new cars to the training camp and start building an army. Sound okay to you?'

Yes sir,' I replied before entering my apartment, however, I wouldn't be waiting till the morning to begin. I grabbed a pen and some paper and began scribbling down names of who I wanted in my army before heading downstairs to try out my new personal training area.

Chapter 20

The following morning after an entertaining drive to camp in my new Mustang Shelby GT500, I stood in the General's office and handed him the list of names I had made the night before.

He took one look at the first name on the list and burst out laughing. 'You sure?' he asked.

'One hundred percent.'

'Alright, let's get started then.'

The General provided me with his own list of armed forces personnel that he assured would not let me down on the battle ground and then we organised a recruiting plan to make up the rest of the numbers. I would not be hand picking all five thousand soldiers but I definitely wanted the best ones for the job and if I could personally choose a decent enough frontline, I'd be happy enough.

The General began making the arrangements to have the names on our list, collected and brought to our own special training camp, and I set forth on a scouting mission.

There was no point wasting my time checking out fully fledged members of the armed forces. The General had the run down on anyone and everyone that had progressed through the training camps and I trusted his judgement, so that angle was covered. I was more interested in the raw recruits. Younger and hungrier for the battlefield perhaps, but you needed physique as well as skill. It would be a step up from the other recruits they were facing on a daily basis so I needed to see them for myself and judge whether they would be up to the task.

The obvious place to start was the gladiator training camp. The best of the best. I picked quite a number from this area for obvious reasons and each and every one of them was delighted to join my ranks. Firstly, it was a great honour to be chosen personally by the champion gladiator to fight for your God and secondly, they were told that if they fought and won, they would be given an immediate promotion into the gladiator ranks on return to camp. It was a no brainer for them really, not that they actually had a choice, but I would always ask first in order to gauge their reaction. I wanted soldiers fighting for me that wanted to be there, not because they had been ordered.

Had anyone refused my offer, I wouldn't have taken them, but I would have had them thrown out of the armed forces and sent to earn their way in some other shithole service for the rest of their days.

Thankfully none did.

Five days later, between the General and I, we had a hand-picked army of 1,256 soldiers. Over the weekend we had the remaining numbers made up by random serving armed forces. The following day, we started training our five thousand strong army.

The next three months proved to be both challenging and hugely enjoyable. Having chosen to avoid bonding and forming friendships in my early gladiator days, I found it was impossible not to in this change of format, despite trying to keep myself slightly distanced, being the leader of the army.

I could definitely see the troops bonding and friendships forming throughout the army.

I now realised that this was probably part of the reason that a great deal of respect was found between fully fledged gladiators. Most of them that lived at least a few years after their debut would have fought in a God's war at some point and bonded in the same way I was witnessing now.

The battle had been arranged on our land, or Cranock's to be exact. There were of course benefits to having the home advantage if you like. However, I have to admit to being a little disappointed we were not travelling to Petra's land as it would have been interesting to see another part of the planet. Something very few humans had the opportunity to do.

Petra's army arrived several days before the battle was due to commence and in a show, mainly for the benefit of the Gods, both armies lined up in formation beside the great pyramid to allow each God to meet and look over the opposition.

I stood at the forefront of my army and silence fell over the land when an announcement rang out, preparing us for the imminent arrival of the Gods.

Two flashes of red light suddenly lit up, then disappeared just as quickly, leaving Cranock and Petra now standing before the two armies.

They moved towards Petra's army first, walking the line of it, pausing to talk briefly with her leader, Petra's champion gladiator. What information had been available had been passed down the ranks in the weeks previously and he came with a big reputation, as you would expect.

As Cranock and Petra now crossed over to our army and started making their way down the line towards me, I suddenly began to feel slightly nervous. It was a daunting thing to meet a God but I had been there already with Cranock and hadn't felt this way so it didn't take a genius to figure out it had something to do with the other God being an extremely good looking female. Deadly of course but beautiful nonetheless.

When they finally paused before me and Cranock introduced me as his champion gladiator, I sank to one knee, as did my army behind me, in a show of respect.

'Rise soldier,' were the first words I heard her say in a voice that matched her appearance. Sultry, sexy and cold. I rose and couldn't help but lock eyes with her as she stood before me, staring into my soul. She was incredibly beautiful, with jet black shoulder length hair, tanned skin and the most amazing green eyes. If she was indeed the double of the old Egyptian Queen Cleopatra, then she too must have been extremely beautiful.

'I've been hearing great things about you, gladiator. High praise from a God is no easy feat.'

'Thank you, your Highness,' I reply, this time ensuring I had been prepped in how I should address our South American Goddess.

'It's almost a shame I'll need to expose all your weaknesses to him tomorrow,' she added coldly.

I glanced at Cranock, unsure what to say, but he just laughed it off saying, 'We'll see,' before urging Petra to continue on their walk down the remaining line of our army.

Petra held my gaze for a further few unnerving moments, before finally joining Cranock once more.

I breathed a sigh of relief as she went. That was intense, I thought to myself, as the sweat dripped down the back of my neck.

Two days later, the two armies stood facing each other once again, except this time only one would be leaving alive.

The Gods always told their armies that anyone left standing on a losing side would be killed by the embarrassed losing God, but they didn't need to as there was never anyone left living on a losing side anyway.

The battles were ferocious and merciless.

An area of open desert had been the spot chosen to fight the battle upon and as we stood in the searing heat, I wondered what effect it might have on either army. The sky was full of black dots which were actually some kind of recording devices that would relay the action to screens across the globe. For the Gods however, nothing but live action would suffice and they had a temporary stand built in the middle of where the two armies stood and where most of the action would likely take place. It was of course built to their luxurious standard and accommodated them and their entourage of servants and high-ranking officials, including the General.

With the moment of truth nearing, I turned to take in the view of my army. They looked ready and hungry for action and glory, especially my number two who stood just behind me.

From the moment I was given the opportunity to assemble my army I knew it would have a place for the old superior guard from the building site. It was the least I could do. I owed him my life. If he hadn't put his neck on the line and offered me a different path in life, I'd still be rotting away on the building sites or worse.

If I'm being honest, I didn't expect to be going into battle with him as my number two. I thought he would have been one of the 'make the numbers up guys' who was really just being granted one last hoorah as I knew he so desired. Clearly the superior didn't see it that way and although a little rusty to begin with, he certainly lacked for nothing in effort. Soon enough he was besting some of the younger gladiators in one on one practise. He truly must have been quite the fighter in his younger days. I couldn't help but be impressed with him as I watched him train and pass his knowledge onto the others, he was a natural leader. In the end it was an easy decision to name him as my number two.

He never actually thanked me for recruiting him to my army, at least not in words, but he didn't need to, you could see it in his eyes and the sheer passion within. The first time I saw him training after arriving, he aimed a curt nod in my direction. That was probably his way of thanking me.

The General said 'Well done,' to me one day as we watched him train with the energy and passion of an up and coming champion. He knew what it meant to the superior.

If there was still any pain or discomfort from the injury that forced him to retire, he certainly wasn't letting it show.

A loud horn sounded and the battlefield fell silent as everyone turned to face the Gods. Cranock stood and addressed the armies with a short speech. I can't really remember what he said as I was too busy staring across the field at the opposing leader and his army, sizing them up and running different scenarios through my head.

I focussed back in when the whole battlefield took to the customary one knee and then listened as Cranock announced, 'On your command leaders, let the battle commence!'

I ordered my army into formation and they immediately took to their feet and readied themselves for battle.

I stood before my men and took a deep breath of air, enjoying one last moment of calm before I unleashed a storm of violence. My body tingled with nervous excitement and adrenaline. I looked up and down the line for the final time, receiving another curt nod from my eager looking number two.

We were primed and ready. This was it!

I stepped forward and yelled 'HONOUR!'

Immediately my five thousand strong army stepped forward one pace and replied at the top of their voices, 'VICTORY!'

I advanced next repeating my call of 'HONOUR!'

As did my army, following with their chorus of 'VICTORY!'

It was something we had planned in advance as a part war cry, part show of respect to Cranock. It may sound a little cheesy, but if you were in my shoes on the battleground and heard five thousand men screaming 'VICTORY!' trust me you'd think otherwise. It sent a tingle down my spine and will stay with me for the rest of my days.

'HONOUR!'

'VICTORY!'

'HONOUR!'

'VICTORY!'

We continued advancing one march at a time. Our counterparts had no such war cry or arrangement and were merely walking towards us as if out for a daily stroll.

'HONOUR!'

'VICTORY!'

A distant yell went up from the opposing leader, signalling for his army to finally erupt in a chorus of noise and begin their charge forward.

There was still a lot of ground between us however, and no need to send my men on a tiring sprint before they engaged in battle, so onward we went with our march.

'HONOUR!'

'VICTORY!'

'HONOUR!'

'VICTORY!'

As Petra's army neared, I finally gave the signal to charge. On my command, instead of yelling 'HONOUR!' I held my sword aloft and screamed at the top of my voice,

'TO VICTORY!'

A blood curdling war cry erupted as the masses reacted to my signal and now charged forward to meet the oncoming horde. I remained still for just a second, savouring the thrill of the moment, but I couldn't wait too long as I wasn't going to let anyone but myself be first into battle.

I set off sprinting to catch up with the frontline and should have known it would be the superior leading the way. I laughed to myself thinking, 'Sorry old man but you're not stealing my leadership charge.'

My pace quickened and I soon passed him to lead the charge. I could almost see the disappointment etched on his face.

Petra's force was close now and I focussed on their illustrious leader. Target the chief and the rest will fall.

Game face on, I pushed myself into top speed and headed straight for him. I imagine he had the same plan, at least to a point. Yards away, I heard him roar as he lifted his sword, readying to strike but instead of doing likewise I tucked mine under my arm and continued forward at top speed.

Battles fought in this nature, when the first collisions took place, soldiers would slow their pace, perhaps only slightly for the more skilled combatants, but all would need to slow at some point in order to wield whatever weapon they were using efficiently.

My opposite number was indeed skilled and didn't require to slow much, but he did just enough for me to take advantage.

I was fast. Very fast. And today that would be my first weapon of choice. I was so fast at top flight I was able to duck my head down and shoulder barge right into their leader before he was able to bring his sword down upon me. He tried, but I was too quick. As his sword came swinging down, the noise of ribs breaking and cartilage crushing, told me I had hit the spot.

His sword fell from his grasp as he let out a horrible sounding groan that signalled his day was over before it had even got started. I continued running like a steam train as his vital organs crushed into my shoulder. Stopping suddenly, I watched as his body flew through the air, before landing like a rag doll on the ground. If he wasn't dead already, he would be soon.

The battleground around me seemed to pause momentarily, as Petra's soldiers looked on in disbelief at what had just happened to their fearless leader.

The shock wore off quickly on the surrounding soldiers and as they descended upon me, I raised my swords and unleashed the full repertoire of my skills, slicing and dicing them up with ease.

This war was already won, they just didn't know it yet.

The battle ended in a landslide victory for our side and would go down in the record books as one of the most crushing, if not *the* most crushing defeat of any army in the history of the Gods' battles. The feeling I felt at the end, topped any gladiator battle I had fought to date. I'd never felt more alive and ecstatic. I was on top of the world and doubted anyone had ever felt as good, well, apart from the old superior maybe.

Chapter 21

The horn eventually sounded once again, signalling us into formation that would allow the Gods to take to the field and congratulate the winners.

As a delighted looking Cranock and not so delighted looking Petra began walking our front line, we took to the customary knee, only rising when they eventually reached myself and instructed us to do so.

'Congratulations on an exceptional display Destroyer,' announced Cranock.

'You have pleased your God greatly today young gladiator and will be duly rewarded. As will your men'

'Thank you, my lord.'

Cranock, then continued moving along the line of men, acknowledging their display on his behalf. Petra's usual cold stare was now decidedly cooler looking, to the point of, if looks could kill.

She made to follow on after Cranock but instead turned back to face myself and stepped in close. Very close.

She stood in silence for a moment, inches from my face, her piercing green eyes once again felt like they were staring into my soul. She was beautiful but also far more intimidating than any of the trained killers that had just graced the bloody battlefield. The wind caught her scent and blew it into my face, sending a rush of the sweetness up my nose and making my mind feel strangely embarrassed about how I must be smelling with a combined nasty fragrance of blood, sweat and dirt.

'Your talent on a battleground is exceptional, gladiator.'

'Thank you, your highness,' I reply feeling extremely uncomfortable.

'You disposed of my champion like he was nothing more than a dirty rag. I'm not sure whether to congratulate you or kill you for embarrassing me like that.'

As I pondered over how best to respond, I was thankfully saved from doing so when Petra made to move away. However, she only managed one step before pausing to turn and look at me once more. I tilted my head slightly and kept my gaze firmly straight and towards the ground in the hope that she would continue on her way.

My plan was quickly thwarted, when I felt the soft touch of her hand on my cheek, drawing my head up until I met her gaze. Her hand stayed on my cheek, whilst her eyes burrowed deep into mine. Her mouth began to open as if she was about to say something when Cranock's voice rang out.

'I hope you're not trying to steal my champion gladiator, Petra. That one's not for sale, at any price.'

Petra drew the North American God a look of scorn, before removing her hand from my cheek and setting off towards him.

Blowing a sigh of relief, I heard the old superior say behind me in a mocking voice.

'I think she likes you.'

I turned and drew him a dirty look in return.

'Can I rub our fearless leader's little cheeky weeky?' he continued in his mocking childish tone, which the surrounding soldiers seemed to find funny as they all began sniggering.

'Shut up,' I say turning once more, only to regret it instantly as for some strange reason I had actually begun to blush and the superior noticed it immediately.

'Everyone, our fearless champion is blushing for his new love, Queen Petra.'

The sniggers grew louder.

How ridiculous can you get? I'd just slayed hundreds of men and stood covered in their blood and guts and yet found myself blushing and being ridiculed by my own men.

'Shut the fuck up before I turn you all red with blood,' I whisper angrily.

Immediately all the soldiers hushed, all bar the superior who continued to snigger away all by himself.

'Prick!'

Chapter 22

After the battle the soldiers were taken back to the training camp to wash and change before returning to the great pyramid to enjoy a celebration feast, courtesy of our God Cranock.

On arrival at one of the great halls where the banquet was being held, as leader I was shown to the table nearest the Gods, who sat together on a raised area nearby, overlooking the masses and unfortunately myself.

I was still feeling conscious of what happened with Petra on the battlefield earlier and a look from the superior with a wry smile as he sat down, told me he hadn't forgotten either.

Keen not to give him anymore ammo to ridicule me with, I kept my gaze firmly away from the Gods' table.

The food that soon arrived was of the finest quality any of us had ever eaten and it was accompanied by another first for most, if not all of us. Wine, and plenty of it.

Alcohol in general was thought to be a distant relic from a bygone era. The Gods had labelled it a poison to humanity that brought about laziness, sickness and violence. Supplies were confiscated and anyone caught making their own moonshine as it was called, was killed.

Surprisingly, people still continued to make their own, despite the risks. It seems humanity's love affair with alcohol was a tough one to break.

When the Gods announced the new tougher sentence of your whole family being sentenced to death if anyone was caught with alcohol, the cord was finally cut. It appeared that the New Earth was finally rid of the human poison and yet here, sitting before two of the very Gods that put the harsh and cruel laws in place, we were being served it in abundance.

It felt wrong and stank of double standards. I refused to drink any and was expecting my army to do likewise. However, as I gazed around the room, I quickly realised that not many seemed to share, or care about my point of view. It was being guzzled down like there was no tomorrow.

'Not thirsty?' asks the superior, pointing towards my empty glass.

'It just doesn't seem right,' I reply.

'No, it probably isn't, but life's too short to worry about the morals kid. Just enjoy it for what it is. You earned it,' he says, picking up one of the bottles and pouring the contents into my cup.

'Come on, raise a glass with me,' he continues. 'Thanks for all this.'

I lifted my glass and smiled, 'Figured I owed you one.'

'That you most certainly did,' he replied laughing.

We chinked glasses then out of curiosity I took a large drink of the wine. If we hadn't been sitting before the Gods, I think I would have spat it out across the table. Instead, I just manged to keep it in my mouth and gulp it down.

'That tastes like piss!' I blurt out, making the superior laugh.

'Yep it sure does,' he replies, 'but after a glass or two, you can't get enough.'

'I'll stick with the water thanks.'

I was just thinking how the Gods had done us a favour taking that away, when I glanced around the room to find that everyone else seemed to share the superior's view of the drink. Most of them would have been like myself and had never tried it before, yet despite its awful taste, they appeared to be thoroughly enjoying it.

The noise level in the room was noticeably getting louder, with many of the soldiers becoming rowdier. This was a recipe for disaster I thought. Survive a God's battle during the day, only to get yourself killed that night for becoming intoxicated and doing or saying something you shouldn't. I wanted out of the place altogether but to get up and leave before the Gods would be seen as disrespectful so I had to sit and grimace for the meantime.

Around an hour later, just as the room felt like it was going to explode, thankfully the Gods made a short speech, then departed to allow the soldiers to continue celebrating by themselves.

I could feel a weight lift off my shoulders as they left. Even the old superior was now rocking and burst into song, much to the delight of the crowd as a huge cheer erupted.

My whole army had gone mad.

Relieved the Gods had left and keen to do the same, I quietly snuck out of the room before anyone caught me and tried to make a scene.

Back in the more peaceful surroundings of my apartment, I relaxed by watching a film on my fantastic new television screen. Once I'd started watching some of the many films it had stored on it, I couldn't stop. Some of them were terrific, some not so much, but either way it was still a great way to unwind and also depending on the film, would give me a glimpse into what life was like before the Gods arrived. I'd watched a film two nights ago that although I really enjoyed, I was still trying to get my head around. It was about time travel in a way and featured a boy who was talking to a freaky looking rabbit at times. Sounds crazy but it was actually very good. Donnie Darko was the title and I'd decided to watch it again to see if I could understand better. It was just as thoroughly enjoyable second time around, but sadly I still hadn't got to the bottom of it.

I'd just turned the screen off and was walking towards the kitchen area, when a blinding red light suddenly lit up the room and the God Petra appeared in its wake.

'Jeez,' I yell, almost having a heart attack. I was about to shout something else but the realisation that it was a God who stood before me kicked in and I just managed to stop myself in time.

'Your Highness, forgive my manners, you just startled me a bit,' I say, taking the customary knee.

'From what I saw today I doubt that happens much gladiator. Rise!' she replies.

Not for the first time today, I was met with that intense stare of hers as I rose to my feet.

'What's your name gladiator? Your real one.'

'Jacob, your Highness.'

'Well Jacob, that was quite the impressive display today,' said Petra as she began to wander slowly around the apartment.

'Thank you, your Highness.'

'You can drop the formalities, for now Jacob, but perhaps your performance was a little too good. Tell me, what's Cranock been supplying you with? Enhancers of some sort?'

'No, your......' I began, finding it strange to drop the formality. 'No, nothing at all. We train hard, fight hard. That's all.'

Petra wandered over to me until she was extremely close once again. Gazing at me with her incredible green eyes, she placed a warm palm on my cheek.

'You wouldn't lie to me now would you Jacob?' she purrs.

'No, I wouldn't,' I answer honestly like a trembling little child. I truly didn't think I could lie to her when she had me like this, even if I wanted to. Her beautiful sultry way, could disarm any man alive and most likely the other Gods as well.

We stood in silence for a moment gazing into each other's eyes, her hand still on my cheek. I was lost in the moment, caught in her spell of beauty. Without thinking, I slowly inched towards her until our lips touched and electricity seemed to shoot through my body. What was I doing? Yet she didn't push me away. We began to kiss slowly. I was in a dream world, with little bombs of pleasure and excitement going off all over my body and then it all ended suddenly with a 'Bang, bang, bang,' on my apartment door.

We broke apart and before I could say anything, I was met with Petra's hand slapping my face, which doesn't sound much but had the impact of being hit with a sledgehammer.

As I stumbled to the side, a flash of bright red light filled the room for a second before disappearing along with the South American Goddess.

'What the fuck just happened?' I think to myself, staring around the room in shock.

Another bang on the door snapped my attention back to that and I quickly jogged over and threw the door wide open to find the General looking back at me with that wry grin of his.

'Congratulations today, boy. Outstanding performance. You'll be in line for a sweet reward for that, let me tell you. I don't think I've ever seen Cranock quite as pleased as he was today.'

'Thank you sir.'

'Well, you going to invite me in or what?'

'Oh yeah, sorry, come in,' I reply moving aside.

As the General walked past, he said, 'You celebrating all by yourself?'

'Trying to,' I mutter under my breath.

'Didn't think you'd stick around down there. It's starting to get messy,' says the General laughing.

'People are going to find themselves in trouble tomorrow the way it was looking when I left.'

'Oh, I'm sure it'll be okay. He tends to be pretty lenient when it comes down to a battle winning celebration, within reason obviously. Anyway, never mind them, I couldn't allow their leader to skulk off by himself without having at least one celebratory drink with me,' replied the General, holding aloft a bottle of dark brown liquid.

'What's that?'

'Whiskey.'

'For a place that banned alcohol, there sure seems to be a lot of it going around.'

The General laughed once again. 'Loosen up champ. Take a look around. You're in the Great Pyramid. You live in the same building as a God. The rules that the masses need to live by out there, don't apply to us in here. Sure, I wouldn't walk around in public with a bottle of whiskey, but in private we can pretty much do what we like. As long as you continue to serve Cranock well and keep him happy, then you're untouchable kiddo. How many people do you see driving around the streets in a Ferrari? In fact, let me put it this way. How many people that aren't gladiators have you ever seen driving?'

I was beginning to realise the General had already drank more than a few whiskeys before he'd arrived at my door. However, he was right. Other than the General himself, I couldn't think of anyone else that got the opportunity to drive around unchecked like we did. 'It just doesn't seem fair,' I finally answer.

'Fair?' scowled the General. 'Don't give me that crock of shit. Life isn't fair. It wasn't fair before the Gods arrived and it still isn't fair now. That's just life. It's what you make of it, life won't do anything for you all by itself. You've got to go out there and grab it by the balls, just like we've done. It might not be fair, but don't tell me we haven't earned what we have now. I put my life on the line on a daily basis to get to where I am, and you still do that. How many ordinary citizens do what you did today for a living?'

He certainly had a point, I'll give him that. As I pondered over his words further, he spoke again.

'Whether it's banned to the masses or not, you've earned your whiskey boy. Now hurry up and get some glasses before I start drinking it straight from the bottle.'

After trying the foul-tasting wine earlier in the evening, I wasn't even remotely interested in trying whiskey now, but trying to argue my point with the already intoxicated

General would probably prove to be even more challenging. So off I wandered to retrieve some glasses for us.

On my way my thoughts turned to Petra. What the heck had happened? Did I fall asleep and dream that? Of all the times for the General to want to share a whiskey with me, it had to happen then.

Perhaps he did me a favour though. Possibly saved my life. Petra was thought of as being the coldest and most ruthless God of them all. Slayer of Men and The Black Widow were among some of the titles she was known by and I had just made a move on her. Or did she make the move on me. Jeez, I couldn't think and a lot could depend on it, like my life for example.

'You lost or something?' yelled the General, snapping me from my thoughts.

I returned with the glasses and grimaced as he poured two very large amounts of whiskey into each glass.

'Cheers,' he says, raising one glass and handing the other to myself.

'Cheers,' I reply, before knocking back the dark liquid.

This time I did spray it across the room.

'What the fuck is that?' I yell incredulously, wiping slabbers of whiskey from my chin. 'That's even worse than the wine. What's wrong with you people? How can you drink that stuff for enjoyment?'

The General was too busy laughing to respond for the time being so I left him to collect some towels to clean up the whiskey that I had just spat across my floor.

'You might be a blood thirsty killer in the arena, but you're a pussy when it comes to drinking,' says the General on my return, much to his own humour.

'Try again?' he asks holding the bottle aloft.

'No thanks, not for me. Today will be my first and last time ever drinking alcohol again.'

'Ach fine, I'll take my bottle somewhere it will be appreciated then. Well done today boy, try to enjoy the moment in some boring way at least. So long pussy,' he adds, before downing the whiskey in his glass and leaving the apartment.

Relieved to gain some peace and quiet once again, I retired upstairs and lay down on my bed. My body was tired from battle but my mind was anything but. All I could think about was Petra. Analysing what happened over and over. She was sultry and beautiful, a cold-hearted killer and an all-powerful God. The question I kept coming back to over and over was, what am I to her?

A potential love interest, her next kill or absolutely nothing at all and I'm just wasting my time over analysing what happened?

Chapter 23

After a restless sleep, I drove to the training camp the following morning in my Ferrari, enjoying the thrill of hitting the top speeds on the deserted highways. There was no requirement to check in to camp today. The soldiers had been given the day off as reward for their victory and to allow them to heal their bodies and no doubt sore heads. Hopefully none of them had lost their heads completely during the night.

Our training area was eerily quiet. Having been used to the noise of five thousand men working hard on a daily basis, it was strange to find it this way. I began exercising and by late morning some of the men had started to appear, most of them in a pitiful state and looking to find a way to rid their bodies of the toxins they had drunk the previous evening.

As I put them through their paces, some ran off to be sick, whilst others just collapsed on the spot, overheating and dehydrating. It was a comical session to say the least and did nothing to enhance my view of alcohol. I was really struggling to understand why it had been so popular pre-God era.

Eventually I called it a day mid-afternoon out of fear of killing anyone and sent them all away to recover. We would have two more days left of our battle camp before everyone returned to duties or started new ones.

Driving back to the great pyramid, I thought about how I would miss the camaraderie of the camp. It had been a refreshing change to be working together instead of the more solitary life of a gladiator. I was also relieved to find that despite some high antics during their party, no one appeared to have stepped too far over the line and was facing any punishment, other than my training session.

My strange encounter with Petra was deemed to be over, forgotten about with her seemingly having returned to her South American base.

I'd be lying if I said there wasn't a little part of me feeling disappointed as she was truly beautiful beyond belief. However, to say that I would be going down an extremely dangerous path mixing with her, would be the understatement of the year, so my relief won over the disappointment.

On return to the pyramid, I ate dinner at one of the high-quality canteens, situated on my level of the building then relaxed in my apartment watching a fantastic film titled Braveheart, which told the supposed true story of a centuries old Scottish war hero called William Wallace.

It was interesting to see how life had been nearly a thousand years ago and left me wondering how much had really changed in all that time. Here we were, fighting in the same manner just yesterday, albeit for very different reasons.

Things change, yet remain the same.

I turned my screen off, pitching the apartment into near darkness and began to make my way to the upper level when that blinding red light suddenly erupted throughout the apartment. As my eyes struggled to re-adjust to the darkness, a cold, sultry voice spoke.

'How dare you insult a God by putting your wretched lips upon mine!'

Oh shit! I think to myself.

'I'm sorry, your Highness. Please forgive me. I meant no disrespect.'

'No disrespect,' she almost spat the words back at me. 'You continue to disrespect me as we speak. Have you forgotten who you stand before?'

I quickly dropped to one knee, rather grudgingly, thinking, perhaps if she didn't keep appearing suddenly in the middle of my apartment, I'd remember my manners better, but wisely chose to keep that thought to myself.

'Get up,' she rasps almost as soon as my knee hits the floor.

The minute I stand she pushes me hard and I fall backwards against the apartment's glass wall. Petra closes the gap between us in the blink of an eye and grabs me by the throat with one hand, pinning me against wall in the process.

Right, God or no God, my patience is wearing thin and I'm about to say something I'll probably regret when she leans in close and plants her lips on mine.

Needs a little work on her foreplay but okay, this is an upturn in events. After a few seconds kissing, I cautiously place my hand on the small of her back and pull her in closer until our bodies are pressed tight against each other. I wait for a reaction like snapping my neck or something equally bad, but it doesn't happen. Quite the opposite. She goes with the flow and our bodies entwine as we begin to tear the clothing from one another.

So engrossed and excited in the moment, I'm not even aware of us moving upstairs, but soon find ourselves on my bed making love. It's the most incredible feeling I've ever experienced and I don't want it to end. Sadly, it eventually does. I open my mouth to say something but she cuts me off by saying 'Silence,' sharply, then climbs out of the bed and disappears in a flash of red light.

I lie back on the bed and laugh with joy and the absurdity of it all. That was the most bizarre and amazing thing that's ever happened to me. God or not, she is the most beautiful woman I've ever encountered, but boy does she need to work on her people skills.

Chapter 24

The next evening Petra appears in my apartment once again and duly leaves just as suddenly as the previous night. Same thing happens the evening after that, only this time as she makes to climb out of the bed, I grab her arm and tell her to wait.

I receive that cold, hard, intimidating stare of hers. However, after being intimate with her for the previous three evenings, its power has been lost on me somewhat.

'Why the need to rush off? Stay a while. Talk to me.'

Without another word, she tears free of my grip and climbs out of the bed.

'If that's the way it is, don't bother coming back,' I say, which draws another look of scorn before she disappears in a blinding flash of red light.

The following night, I found myself pacing the apartment wondering whether the Goddess would be making an appearance or not. Time dwindled by slowly before I decided to take my mind off the matter by watching a film. My plan didn't have the desired result as I found myself unable to free my thoughts of her and by the time the film ended I couldn't even have told you what the story was about. I stayed up later than usual, sub-consciously hoping for the sultry Goddess to appear, but she never did.

Three more days and nights came and went without any signs of her returning. I couldn't stop thinking about her, even when training during the day and was cursing myself for what I'd said. I should have been more patient. If all she wanted was sex, would that really have been such a bad thing?

Convinced I had blown it, I was feeling rather glum as I gazed out from my apartment at the spectacular view of the sun setting, when the darkness behind me lit up in a red glow. I spun around immediately to find Petra standing before me, looking as beautiful and mysterious in the dark light as she ever had. The Egyptian style gold make up she wore around her eyes reflected off the last rays of sunshine that streamed through the glass, complimenting her sparkling green eyes.

'Well? What do you want to talk about?' she demanded.

I couldn't help but laugh which I don't think was the reaction she was expecting.

'Are you mocking me now?'

'No, of course not,' I say raising my palms in an apologising gesture. 'I'm sorry, I didn't mean to laugh at you. I'm glad you're here. I missed you.'

This seemed to please her and douse the spark of annoyance that was beginning to grow within.

'Let's talk about anything.'

'Alright,' she replied, before we both fell into a long silence as my mind went blank and for some reason, I couldn't think of a single thing to say. The silence was becoming awkward, but the harder I tried to think of something to talk about, the less came to mind.

Petra turned away and began to wander around the apartment, pausing to look at the large screen, which thankfully gave me an idea.

'Do you watch films?' I ask, breaking the silence.

'Films?' she replies, raising an eyebrow.

'Films. Or movies? You watch them on the screen for entertainment. At least, most humans did before you arrived.'

'I know what you refer to but I have never viewed any films or movies as you call them.'

'I've only just discovered them myself. They're actually pretty enjoyable. Would you like to watch one?'

Petra looked towards me looking a little unsure, before eventually agreeing.

'Please, have a seat,' I said, motioning towards the large couch in front of the screen.

What kind of film do you play for an all-conquering, all-powerful, beautiful but deadly Goddess? That was the next problem I faced. Not an easy choice.

I finally picked one that I had particularly liked titled Forest Gump, which raised an eyebrow or two from Petra when it began. Thankfully as I had done, she soon became engrossed in the story, laughing almost uncontrollably at parts. It was the first time probably anyone on Earth had seen her laugh like this. It was nice and made it seem for a while at least, like we were just a normal couple enjoying each other's company. During the film, we moved closer, our hands entwining before soon I held her in my arms as we cuddled together. I'm sure I almost saw a tear in her eye as the film reached one of its sadder points. When it ended, she turned her head to mine and we kissed.

Before long, we found ourselves in bed again, yet she showed no desire to leave this time and remained beside me when I eventually drifted off to sleep.

I awoke sharply in the morning and rolled over expecting to find an empty bed but was delighted to find her lying awake beside me.

'Morning,' I say smiling.

'Morning,' she replies, returning the smile too.

The sheets lay at her waist, showing off her lovely tanned skin and body. Her face, every bit as beautiful as it looked the night before.

'I need to go now,' she whispers softly.

I nod sadly. 'Come back tonight?'

It was her turn to nod this time, 'I will.' We then kissed, before she climbed out of bed and disappeared in the usual fashion. I lay back on the bed with the largest grin on my face.

A short while later, a loud knock on my apartment door got me out of bed. I ran downstairs to answer it, finding the General there, looking to see if I was in the mood for a race to training camp in one of our many high-performance vehicles.

I was always game for a race, so invited him in to wait whilst I got myself ready. Had I been paying more attention whilst running to answer the door I would have noticed, as the General just had, various items of Petra's clothing lying around.

'Got some company, have we?' he asks with a sly grin.

I ignored the question whilst I gathered up the clothing as quickly as possible.

'Ooooh very nice. Must be high class wearing something as fancy as this!' said the General, holding aloft a jewel encrusted silk top that Petra had been wearing.

The smile suddenly vanished from the General's face as the realisation of how very few people in the world would own something like that kicked in.

'Jacob, whose top is this?'

'None of your business,' I reply yanking it from his grip.

'Is she still upstairs?' he continues in a low whisper.

'No, there's no one here but me, now let it go. I'll be ready in ten minutes.'

I rushed off upstairs before the General could enquire any further, and threw Petra's clothes into a cupboard that was now gathering a collection of them. It made me wonder where she went after leaving my apartment, as each time she left, she would climb out of bed naked and disappear without collecting her clothes.

After a quick shower and change, we left the apartment and were taking the elevator to the parking level, when the General spoke again.

'Just tell me she's single and you're not messing around with anyone's partner Jacob. You know the rules and the punishment.'

'Relax sir, she's single. I'm not messing around with anyone's partner. Why would you think that in the first place?'

'How many single women do you see wearing clothes as fine as that round these parts?'

He was right of course. I'm not sure how things were under Petra or Ti'ar's rule, but there were very few high-ranking positions of power for females under Cranock's roof. Most of the ones dressed in fine clothing were partners of high ranking, male officials and even fewer, if any, would be wearing something encrusted with so many lavish jewels. Only Cranock's *special* servants would perhaps be rewarded with such lavish clothing and to be caught sleeping with one of them would be viewed as an insult of the highest order. Of course, the only other person you would find in this type of garment would be a Goddess. I doubt he would think for a second that was a possibility, but I could see his point.

'What's the choice of vehicles today?' I ask, keen to change the subject.

'I'm thinking the Lamborghini and the Dodge Viper?' replies the General. The thought of trying out some of the new cars we had acquired as reward for winning the recent battle, returned a smile to his face.

'Sounds good to me.'

The General sure loved his cars and thankfully the exhilarating drive to camp seemed to have taken his mind off the matter of my new lover. I also eased off the gas to ensure he won that day. I didn't like to lose at anything, but the sacrifice to ensure he arrived at camp in a good mood worked and left me to train hassle free for the remainder of the day.

On return to the great pyramid, I was pleased to find Petra making herself at home in my apartment, as she lounged on the couch watching Forest Gump again. Over the next two months we saw each other every single night and I was very quickly falling deeply in love with her.

One evening as I stroked her naked back whilst we lay in bed, I decided to ask the question I had been thinking about for a very long time.

'What are you Petra?' I whisper softly.

'What?' she replies, turning to look me in the eyes.

'What are you?' I repeat.

She gave me a strange look this time before saying, 'You know what I am.'

'But are you really? That's what I'm asking. Are you and the others really Gods?

She pulled away from me, scowling as if I had just deeply offended her.

'Are you trying to mock me?'

'No, not at all. I don't care whether you are a God or not. I'm just trying to find out more about the person I've fallen in love with.'

Petra had now completely backed off out of the bed, looking shocked as she stood, covering herself with the bed sheets.

'You can't say that. You can't fall in love with me.'

'Why not? Surely you must feel something too?'

Petra shook her head slowly, looking lost for words, before she began to move further from the bed. I'd seen this move before and knew exactly what was about happen.

'Don't go! Not now, please,' I shout, but in the blink of an eye, she was gone. I fall back on the bed exasperated. Gods were hard work!

Chapter 25

Petra did not appear the following evening, or the next. On the third day since I had last seen her, I was informed by the General of my next gladiator fight. It was an interesting one. Apparently my displays, particularly in the recent battle against Petra's army, had not gone unnoticed by the other Gods watching that day.

Cero, the presumed leader of the Gods had laid down the challenge of fighting his champion. A best of the best contest.

Despite the fact it would be me, fighting to the death in the arena, Cranock would probably gain more from my victory than anyone else. Claiming the scalp of Cero's champion would be a first for any of the other Gods. Cero remained undefeated, not only with his champion gladiators, but also in the epic war battles between the Gods too, of which was to follow the gladiator contest if I was successful.

'Win both of them and you'll definitely be moving right to the top of the pyramid,' joked the General. In truth however, he probably wasn't far off the mark.

News of the contest was a welcome distraction from my constant thinking about Petra and I threw myself into training with a renewed vigour. Yet she remained at the back of my mind all day and very much at the forefront of it all evening.

Not for the first time, I feared I would not see her again, but thankfully, once again, she returned. Nine days later, the apartment lit up red and I jumped up off the couch, unable to hide my delight at her re-appearance.

'This is not going to be easy. I tried to rid you from my thoughts but I cannot. I too have developed weak, human feelings towards you,' said Petra.

'Such romantic words,' I joke, producing a scowl from her. 'Is that your way of saying you love me?'

'Perhaps. But before we move forward, I will answer your question of what I am, and see if you still feel the same way. Agreed?'

'Of course,' I reply, suddenly feeling some rare nerves.

'Come then,' she says holding out her hands.

I walk closer and accept them, entwining our fingers together. As we gaze into each other's eyes, the slightest of smiles forms on her mouth, right before everything turns bright red.

Chapter 26

It's hard to describe the feeling, but it's definitely not a good one. When the red light disappears, I drop to my knees and wretch.

'Are you alright?' I hear Petra ask.

I felt like someone had just stuck their hand right down my throat and pulled my innards out. Rather than saying that however, I just held a finger aloft in the universal sign for saying, give me a minute.

'It's been so long now I forget what it was like the first time I did it, but it does get easier.'

A few deep breaths and a moment or two later, I wearily rise to my feet and take in my new surroundings.

Petra now stood about thirty yards away, before a large, dark window. It could have just been the time of night making it look so dark beyond the window, but I doubted it. Wherever I was, it looked nothing like I had ever seen on Earth. In the middle of the room, holograms or 3-d images of planets and galaxies hung mid-air. The floors and walls almost matched the darkness of beyond the window, and were sleek and polished looking.

'Join me,' said Petra. Keeping her gaze upon me as I slowly began walking towards her. The holograms or whatever they were, kept changing into different planets and galaxies as I passed by. Nearing Petra, I now noticed a glow coming in from the dark window. A light source of some sort, but as she smiles at me and holds her hand out, my gaze stays firmly on her mesmerizing and beautiful eyes, rather than what was beyond the window.

I take her hand and we both turn to face the view together. Part of me is in shock and awe and the other part of me feels like it is finally getting confirmation of something I had suspected all my life. The glow came from a distant planet, we were looking down upon. A very recognisable planet and one that I called home.

From where I stood at the large window, I was able to look around and see a great deal of the vessel I was now a passenger on. It was huge and I was only seeing part of it. A grand spaceship, befitting of one of the recent films I had watched, like Independence Day or Star Wars.

'So, you're not a God then?' I ask, turning to face Petra.

'That depends. You have to ask yourself, what is a God really? A superior being compared to a human? Then yes, you could argue the case reasonably well. If you are asking, did we create human life, then no, but that's not even a relevant question as that type of God does not exist. There does exist, many other inhabited planets, hundreds, possibly thousands that we know of across the millions of other galaxies out there.

Humans are so ignorant and self-absorbed that many believe they are the only beings to exist. This is despite having at least a basic understanding of the sheer vastness of space. Yet still, they want to stay in their little bubble of believing they are special and in God, and that they alone were created by the almighty.

'Bit of a generalisation, is it not?' I state.

Petra places her hand on my cheek. 'You know I don't mean you and yes, not all humans feel or think this way, but most of them do. We watched and studied Earth for a very long time before showing ourselves. Humans want

God in their lives. Crave it even, and so, we gave them what they wished for.'

I took a moment to absorb Petra's words, turning to gaze out across the darkness of space towards the planet of our discussion.

Eventually facing her again I ask, 'So who exactly are you and where are you from? Forget Earth and all the other humans. It's just me asking. The man who has fallen deeply in love with you.'

It was now Petra's turn to take a moment before answering.

'We are from a planet and galaxy so far from Earth you would struggle to comprehend the distance. As a species we are far more evolved, advanced and intelligent than humans are currently, but they are not the worst. There are many other civilisations and human like species out there, some highly advanced and intelligent and others basic and primitive. Earth's inhabitants lie around halfway, if you were to measure it on a scale. Somewhat advanced and intelligent, yet their inability to rid themselves of the need for conflict and war with each other, still holding them back from truly evolving as a species, to the point where they were killing not only the planet but themselves in the process.

Our actions saved both from extinction.'

'I'm not sure that's a view most humans would share,' I say.

'Only because they are too weak minded to accept the truth. The planet as a whole knew it was over populated and yet failed to act. The opposite in fact, allowing over breeding to continue at a ridiculous rate. Everyone knew the planet was being drained of its minerals and resources and what did they do about it? Nothing! Global warming, the ozone layer, flooding and fires on grand scales. The planet was practically slapping them in the face to take action, but no one did.

Truly advanced species can make the hard decisions and act upon the signs. Earth's humans were, and probably always will be, too obsessed with greed and war to ever advance on their own. They had reached their peak as a species and were on a path of self-implosion before we arrived.'

'Why did you arrive? If we disgust you so much as species, why save us, as you put it?' I ask, sounding more than a little irked.

Petra smiles. 'Don't take it personally Jacob. Humans don't disgust me, they just have many faults. You wanted to know the truth and that is what I am telling you, but the human in you is doing what humans do. Take offence too easily, and then turn to conflict. Would you prefer me to stop and return to Earth?'

'No, I'm sorry, you're right. I want to know, please continue,' I reply, now feeling rather silly.

'Very well. To answer your question, we simply needed a new home. We have been exploring the solar system for a very long time and are well beyond the means of ever returning to our home planet. Our ship's power source is depleted to such a level, it is now unable to travel beyond the speed of light, which enabled us to travel so far into the depths of space. It is not a surprise however. Our mission of exploration was always a one-way ticket, as you humans like to say.

And while there are many other species and civilisations in the greater space, none dwell within any of Earth's nearest galaxies.

So, having found ourselves nearby with a limited fuel source, it was a simple option. Make a new home on Earth or die a long slow boring death aboard our ship. We spent a long time observing the planet before making our arrival. Advanced technology allowing us to remain hidden while we did so. Even before our arrival, unmanned smaller vessels have been watching over Earth and many other planets for a very long time. Recording and sending data to us before we had even left our home planet. We were probably not the only ones doing so either.'

'I'm guessing most of the landing day destruction was courtesy of this ship we're on now?'

'It was. While it may not have the fuel levels required to travel beyond light speed, it still has the power to function in every other capacity for the foreseeable future.'

'How long is that exactly?'

'Hundreds of years. If it remains in its current semi-dormant state, possibly thousands.'

'Couldn't you have made a new home on Earth peacefully? Spread your knowledge and taught us how to become a better species?'

Petra gave me a knowing look. 'You didn't witness life before we arrived. It was chaos and they weren't even aware of it. Humans were out of control. The planet was over populated, over drained and dying. Hard decisions had to be made for the greater good. Decisions humans were unable to make, too caught up in their own ridiculous laws that they preached with one hand and broke with the other. Humans wouldn't change the peaceful way and had to be taught a lesson. A reckoning with God or in our case Gods.

The population needed culled and for those that remained, much guidance to say the least. That is what we have done. Gods or not, the point could be argued, but we are superior in every way. Why would or should we sit on an even keel with such a small minded, greedy, conflict driven species?'

'Don't hold back now,' I retort, half laughing.

'It's the simple truth. And now you know.'

'Yeah I guess I do,' I reply slowly, gazing into space once more as I tried to take it all in.

After a minute or two I ask, 'How does this whole red light, transporting, disappearing thing work? Do you just press a button or something?'

This time Petra laughed. 'It's a little more technical than that, but also in a way, yes.'

'Where is it then?' I say, looking around. 'I've seen pretty much all there is to see of you and I haven't once seen any button of sorts.'

Petra shook her head. 'You never will. The technology is inside us. Like a tiny super computer, implanted in our brain that allows us to do many things, including the red-light transportation, as you put it.'

Do you just ask it to transport you somewhere and it does?'

'In a way, yes.'

'Anywhere?'

'It has limits. Going to another planet or galaxy from here would be too far, but anywhere on Earth is within reach.'

I became lost in my thoughts for a few minutes until Petra broke the silence.

'Do you still love me?'

'What?.......Yes….of course.'

'Despite what you now know?'

'I won't lie, it's a lot to take in, but my feelings for you haven't changed a bit. If anything, I love you more for being honest with me.'

Petra moved towards me, her face inches from mine.

'I am glad to hear that. For I too am in love with you,' she says before we begin kissing passionately.

When we eventually break apart, I ask, 'What now? Will the other Gods know what you have shown me? Can I leave Cranock's service to be with you?'

'Cero will soon, for sure. He was the leader of our mission and this vessel and has remained in that position since forging a new life for ourselves on Earth. His implant is linked in with our ship's mainframe, more than any of the rest of us, so he will be aware of your presence aboard.

I plan to speak with him regarding our relationship anyway, so that is not a concern. What is however, is freeing you from Cranock's service. Upon deciding to make Earth our new home we agreed that maintaining control over the planet would be easier if we split up and each presided over certain areas, which roughly amounted to the five most heavily populated continents. Each God would rule over their area and anything within it, including the humans. Any disagreements, would be

put to Cero as ultimate leader, to decide upon, which of course, means you are Cranock's by right. If you were just a regular soldier, I'm sure he would be open to negotiating to allow you to move under my rule.
But you're not just any regular soldier, are you?'
I shrug my shoulders sheepishly.
'You are his champion gladiator of course, and not only that, you're the best he's ever had and he knows it.'
'Aaaaw thanks,' I jest.
'Lap it up, but being the best doesn't help us right now.'
'Oh, I see.'
Cranock knows you are special and he won't want to let his prized possession go, particularly with the upcoming contest against Cero's champion. We Gods take great pride in our contests against one another and Cero's gladiators remain undefeated, as does he in the war battles between Gods. Defeating Cero's champion, will be like Cranock defeating Cero himself in the arena.
And if he then backs that up with a subsequent war battle victory, Cranock will see himself as the new leader among us. That is what you give him. The chance to become the God of Gods.'

'For having such a dim view of humans, strength aside, it doesn't sound like we are that different.'
Petra smirks. 'Yes, perhaps you have a point, but let me say this. As a species, we have changed for our time spent on Earth. Living as a God, ruling over mankind as we do. It changes you. This is not how we used to be and we have become spoiled with our ways on the New Earth as we labelled it. We immersed ourselves into the human way of life and now we are paying the price. For greed

and conflict, humankinds' biggest fault, has now become ours too. Is that our fault, or merely an unavoidable consequence of when two alien species become one?'

'It seems a little harsh to blame the occupants of a planet that you invaded, for giving you all God like egos.'

'Yes, I see your point, but I do not mean to cast blame. Our fault, their fault, it does not matter, I am merely stating what is.'

'How far will Cranock go? Would the Gods ever actually kill each other in a quest for more power?'

'Unless something changes dramatically in our current way of living, then I think it is not a case of if, but when. We spend so much time apart in our own territories, being treated as Gods, you forget what it's like to have to follow an order. It doesn't happen often, but from time to time, Cero will make a demand of someone and it can be very hard to come down from your lofty position and do as he commands.

I know that may sound very small and inconsequential, but often it is the smallest things that lead to the largest conflicts. Humankind's history is littered with evidence of this.

Also, not all of us need to suddenly decide to want to bid for ultimate glory. It only requires one little seed of doubt to spark all-out war. For example, I do not harbour any ambitions of becoming the god of Gods. I do however, feel threatened by Cranock's craving for ultimate power. Fear enough to strike first? Perhaps not just yet, but I may change my mind soon.

If war began between us, I'm sure the other Gods would get involved. Sides would be drawn, alliances may change, partners double crossed, until only one God remains.

Therefore, I believe it is inevitable that the Gods will eventually war with each other. It could happen tomorrow or it could be another thirty years from now or even one hundred years, but ultimately, it will happen.'

'Well the future sounds just rosy,' I say sarcastically.

'It also may never happen, but only if we change in some way,' replied Petra, as her sparkling green eyes stared deep into mine.

'So what now?' I ask.

'Now I speak to Cranock. Not that I expect him to be obliging, but that is how I must proceed. Once he refuses, I will then take my request to Cero, who will listen more reasonably and make the final decision.'

'And if he refuses your request too?'

'Let us wait and see what happens first before answering that question.'

'Okay fair enough, but what do I do meantime?'

'Carry on as normal as best you can. Once I make our feelings known to Crannock, he will most likely feel you have betrayed him. Thankfully, you are too valuable to him right now for him to kill you, but his attitude towards you may become hostile to say the least. If you can avoid him for the time being, I would.'

'Duly noted,' I reply.

'Shall we return now?'

I nod my head and Petra holds out her hands for me to take. I look at the view once again for a moment before accepting them and becoming engulfed in red light.

Chapter 27

When Petra left my apartment the following morning, she promised she would speak to Cranock very soon and inform me as soon as she had. I spent the day training, but with other thoughts consuming my head, for the first time in my life, I found I was relieved to finish for the day and return to the great pyramid.

My hopes of finding Petra awaiting my arrival with good news were short lived, finding only an empty apartment on my return. The clock ticked slowly by, as the night came and went without any news from Petra.

I struggled half-heartedly through training once more, at a time when I should be giving my all with potentially my hardest gladiator fight so far, just around the corner. I couldn't help it though. Since joining the armed forces and rising through the ranks, I never had anything else to distract me really. My goal was clear and becoming a gladiator was the only thing I desired. I had no fear and nothing to lose. Now, all of sudden, everything had changed. Something else, or rather someone else, consumed my thoughts and desires. I loved being the champion gladiator and lived for the fight. The euphoric feeling of performing in the arena was unbelievable and yet when I asked myself if I would give it all up and walk away from the glory to be with Petra, the answer was yes.

Unfortunately that outcome was out with my control and another long, frustrating night lay ahead of me. Morning arrived, still with no contact from Petra.

Thankfully when I returned from training later that day, I was greeted by the alluring sight of her.

'Well?' I enquired.

'Don't get excited,' she replied, dashing my slim hopes of Cranock being reasonable over the situation.

We embraced and kissed, which helped to lift my spirit before Petra continued. 'I'm sorry for being out of contact for so long. Cranock reacted exactly as I expected, badly. I therefore had to visit Cero, who was most interested in you and asked that I remain in Europe for a few days whilst he investigated the matter and spoke to Cranock.

The outcome or rather lack of outcome, was that nothing would be decided until after your contest with his champion and subsequent war battle. Should you still remain alive and well after this, Cero will make a decision then.'

'I see,' I say rather disheartened. 'I guess it's better than a straight no.'

'Perhaps. However, should you win both contests for Cranock, I fear Cero may have other things to worry about than this and potentially it might not be his decision to make anymore.'

'It shouldn't be anyone's decision but ours,' I say angrily. 'Why don't we make it ours and just go. Do your red light thingy and take me to South America with you. If Cranock wants to come after us, let him.'

'I admire your bravery. However, if we were to do that, we would be held accountable by the remaining four Gods, not just Cranock. You would be sentenced to death and I would be given a warning and ordered to hand you over. Failure to comply would eventually lead to death for both of us.'

'So be it. They might find it harder to kill us both than they think.'

'Oh I'm sure they would, but unfortunately it would not be contested in the close combat manner you are accustomed to. The strike would come from above, from the vessel you were aboard three nights ago. The same kind of strikes that wreaked havoc on Earth when we announced our arrival on the planet. We would be obliterated before we even knew what was happening.'

'Can you not do something to the ships mainframe that disables the weapons?'

'I could if we had another God on our side. Any use of weapons or system overrides, requires the clearance of two Gods.'

'Would a dead God help?' I ask, making Petra give me a strange look. 'As in, how does the clearance work? Could you do it if we killed Cranock for example and took him to the ship with us?'

Petra laughs. 'So keen to kill a God now are we?' she asks, placing a hand on my cheek.

'A fake God,' I reply.

'My dear, God or not, we are still a far superior species in so many ways to humans, do not take lightly the thought of fighting Cranock. You are very talented indeed, but he would be on a different level to anyone you have ever faced before. We just need to be a little patient for now. Save your focus for Cero's champion and make sure you win that fight first before thinking about aiming higher.'

I let the matter go for the time being and we tried to take our minds off the subject by watching a film aptly titled – Gladiator. It was a great movie albeit the wrong time to watch it as the film revolved around a champion gladiator being screwed over by the region's ruler and ultimately killed. It didn't take a stretch of the imagination to see the comparisons.

In the morning Petra parted ways with a final warning for me.

'Be wary of Cranock. It benefits him to keep you alive to fight for him, but that doesn't make you invincible. He can be unpredictable at times and may change his mind over keeping you around at any point.'

'Don't worry, I'll be fine,' I reply, kissing her before she disappears.

Arriving at training camp later that morning, I took Petra's advice and focussed my energy on the upcoming battle with Cero's champion. It led to a far more productive day's training than the previous few had been and I returned to the pyramid at night feeling invigorated once more.

Entering my apartment, I heard music playing and looked towards the screen, expecting to see Petra. I was instead greeted by the sight of the General sitting on my couch. He turned the music off immediately and turned to face me.

'A God?'

'Sorry?' I reply.

'An actual God? Of all the women you could have slept with, you had to choose an actual God!'

I shrug my shoulders. 'Why not?'

'Cause it's fucking dangerous you idiot!' spits the General, rather angrily, which makes me laugh.

'Alright, calm down. I've never seen any rules forbidding it and it's better than sleeping with someone's partner, which you thought I was doing.'

'I wish it was someone's partner now. I could have got you out of that at a push, but this is well beyond my control.'

I walk towards the General and place my hand on his shoulder.

'Thank you sir, I appreciate your concern and everything you have done for me, but I wouldn't ask for or expect you to intervene in this matter.'

'Listen to me son. You're playing with fire here. Cranock is fuming and if you were anyone other than who you are, you'd be dead already.'

'Yeah, so everyone keeps telling me, but I've no regrets. I love Petra and I'm willing to take my chances on what happens next. Let Cranock fume all he wants,' I reply walking towards the kitchen area to fetch a drink.

'I'm afraid a friendly chat is not the only reason I'm here,' says the General, making me pause mid step.

'Oh yeah! What's the other reason then?'

'He wants you out of the apartment.'

'What?' I reply, despite hearing fine well what the General said.

'He wants you out of the apartment. Or I should say, he wants you out of the pyramid altogether.'

'And where exactly am I being moved to?'

'Back to the basic units for newly graduated gladiators.'

'My cars?'

The General shakes his head. 'Gone too, I'm afraid.'

I take a deep breath, then laugh sarcastically. 'After all I've done for that ungrateful sack of shit.'

The General's face turns to one of shock. 'Jeez, watch what you're saying son. There's eyes and ears everywhere.'

'Good! I hope he's listening,' I reply.

'Talk like that is a death sentence on its own.'

'Everything I do these days seems to be worthy of a death sentence,' I scoff. 'I've done everything he's ever asked of me and more, and this is how I am treated?'

'Keep your head down and behave and you'll be back before you know it.'

'Behave?' I say incredulously. 'I wasn't aware I had misbehaved in the first place.'

'You know what I mean.'

'Yes, I know exactly what you mean. Put my life on the line and kill for my master's pleasure and benefit,' I say shooting the General a look of scorn, despite knowing it's not his fault.

'What can I say kid, he's a God.'

'Hah! He's no God. He's a fucking hypocrite! That's what he is.'

'Look, get your stuff together and we'll get out of here before you land yourself in real bother. We can discuss the matter further in private, enroute to camp.'

'No, I don't think I'll do that.'

'I know you're angry son, but this isn't a request, it's an order. Now get your shit together.'

'Where is he?'

'What?'

'You heard. Where is he?'

'Don't be stupid boy.'

'Where is he? He talks about loyalty and honour, but where is his? He wants to cast me aside, purely for falling in love, yet still expects me to perform for him. Does that sound honourable to you?'

I march for the front door. 'You can either take me to him or I can run amok through this entire pyramid until I find him.'

Pausing at the door, I turn to see the General with his face in hands. 'I'm asking as a friend. Please don't do this.'

'Don't worry, this isn't on your hands, but it's happening one way or the other. Are you taking me or not?'

The General shook his head, before finally moving towards me. 'See if I end up in the shithole next to you, it'll be me killing you, not him.'

'Thanks sir,' I reply smiling.

A short while later, we had travelled to the higher echelons of the great pyramid and were standing before a large double door.

'You absolutely sure, this is what you want to do?' ask's the General.

'One hundred percent. By the sounds of it, I'll be lucky to ever set foot in the pyramid again, so this might be the one and only chance I get to speak to him.'

The General shook his head in dismay. 'Alright, will you at least wait here a minute and let me tell him that you wish to talk?'

'Fair enough, but if he says no, I'll be going in regardless.'

'Okay, give me a minute then,' replied the General before he knocked on the large door, waited a few seconds, then entered.

Now standing alone in the deafeningly quiet corridor, doubt began to creep into my head. Was I really just about to question a God's actions to his face?

Remember, he's not a God. But perhaps that fact was giving me a foolish sense of over confidence. As Petra had pointed out, God or not, they were still far superior and advanced than humans.

Did he really need me to fight Cero's champion or was I relying on that too heavily. Was I pushing his patience too far?

The door opened suddenly, breaking me from my thoughts.

'Cranock will see you now Jacob,' said the General sullenly.

Time to find out, I think, entering the room.

Cranock stood at the far side of a rather empty and spacious room, with one wall made of dark glass, much like my apartment, only larger and at a higher level. A viewing gallery of sorts, quite spectacular I'm sure, but I wasn't here to admire the view. Noticing my entrance, he cast aside the servant he had been busy speaking to, who rather hastily exited via another door at their side of the room.

Cranock remained still, eyeballing me as I walked towards him. The door banging shut behind me, made me glance around to see the General had stayed in the room but appeared to be waiting by the door.

I stop about ten yards from Cranock and bow my head, 'My lord.' Decorum would normally have me taking a knee and rising only when instructed to do so, but this was all the respect I was willing to muster today.

Cranock remained silent.

'My lord, I feel I am being unfairly punished for a lack of loyalty and honour when I have shown you nothing but.'

'Is that right?' sneers Cranock, finally breaking his silence.

'All my victories have been in your name and there's no reason for that to stop. I would be prepared to continue fighting on your behalf, if you would allow my relationship with Petra to continue without fear of intrusion or retribution. We can all benefit from this situation before Cero has to make a decision that will ultimately upset someone.'

Cranock began to laugh.

'We're negotiating now are we? You forget your place in the world boy! Perhaps sleeping with a God has foolishly made you think you are one.'

In the blink of an eye, Cranock made up the ground between us and grabbed hold of my throat, with a vice like grip. Damn he was quick.

'You are but a speck of dirt on my sole. You do not offer me terms. I order and you obey. You belong to me, not Petra. Do not concern yourself with Cero's decision. He does not rule this land, I do! It doesn't matter what he decides, there is only one God in this room and you will do as I command or die!'

As Cranock squeezed my neck even tighter, my anger came rushing back and I grabbed his arm with both of mine and yanked it free from my neck.

'There's no God in this room,' I spit back at him.

The look of shock and anger at me having the audacity to aggressively touch a God and speak so dis-respectfully towards him, was plain to see on Cranock's face.

Fire flashed within his eyes as he stepped forward and placed his hands on my chest, pushing me backwards with a force unlike any I had felt before.

Both feet left the ground as I sailed backwards, before landing roughly on the floor, not far from the General. I immediately spring to my feet, growling, ready to engage. This wasn't quite how I envisaged things going down, but so be it. Time to find out just how superior or God-like they really are. I could hear the General shouting something, but it was just background noise now. My focus was on the main threat in front of me. With no weapons, it would be a plain hand to hand combat, which I hoped would be to my advantage.

That thought didn't last long however, as Cranock reached into his pocket and removed a small object. Holding it in his palm, it appeared to glow blue, before growing exponentially, until it formed into the long, thick, club like weapon, Cranock was known for using. 'Shit!'

Cranock's face bore a snarling grin as he now sprang towards me, weapon at the ready. Suddenly a bright red light flashed between us and Petra appeared, immediately drawing her large daggers.

'Leave him be Cranock!' she yelled.

'He raised his hand to a God. He deserves to die,' Cranock replied with venom.

'With good reason I'm sure. Kill him and it will be viewed as an act of war against me.'

'And what if I want a war against you?' Cranock says with a wry smile.

'Give me a weapon Petra, I'll fight him just now,' I intervene.

'SHUT UP,' Petra snarls back at me with such anger I fear her more than Cranock, who is now laughing.

'I'm sure you do want war, but are you ready for one against us all?' says Petra.

The Gods stared in silence at each other for a moment before Cranock said,

'Are you really choosing a human over your own kind?'

'View it however you like Cranock, but he is not to be harmed.'

'And since when did I start taking orders from you? He replies. 'This is my land and by agreement, I own all that resides within it. Your young fighter here belongs to me and I will do as I see fit with him.'

'It is to your benefit that he lives also. Let him go free today and he will honour you with victory on Saturday against Cero's champion. We both know how much you want that. It's only two days away, why ruin your chance of glory now over a trivial matter of ego?'

Cranock turned away and began to pace back and forward across the room as he thought over Petra's words. When he came to a halt, his weapon glowed blue for a moment, before retracting into the small shaped object it had initially been in the palm of his hand. Cranock slipped it into his pocket before addressing Petra.

'Very well. You have my word that I will not harm your precious human here between now and the fight. I can give you no guarantees after that. If ever a great performance was needed to please your God, it is now,' he adds looking towards me.

I could think of a few choice words of reply but thought better of it and remained silent instead.

Petra slid her daggers from sight as she turned around, but rather than talking to me, she looked at the General and said, 'Get him out of here now!'

The General immediately walked over to me and grabbed my arm, trying to pull me away. 'Come on Jacob.'

I remained firm and resisted until Petra's fiery gaze fell upon me and she barked, 'Go now, before we both change our minds.'

With that I finally relent and leave the room with the General.

Chapter 28

'Well that went well,' the General says sarcastically, as we travel down the great pyramid in one of its many elevators.

I smile sheepishly at him. 'Sorry.'

He just shakes his head and sighs.

Realising we have passed by the floor of my apartment, I say, 'I need to collect my belongings.'

'I'll get your belongings later. I think it's best for all concerned that we get you as far away from here as possible,' replies the General.

He probably had a point. Not long later, I watched the great pyramid fade into the distance in the rear view mirror, as the General put his foot to the floor and sped us away from the building. Few words were spoken during the journey and when we arrived back at the camp I dove straight into some training. There was no need to check out my new accommodation. I knew exactly what it would be like and I had nothing to even put in it at this point anyway. The training area was relatively quiet, with most of the fighters now resting after a hard day's work out. The few that were around probably regretted going for extra practise that night, as I soon put them to use, taking out my frustrations in a rather heavy handed, sparring session.

Several hours later, the tired and beaten gladiators around the room were shocked when the centre of the hall suddenly lit up in an electrifying burst of red light, as Petra appeared. They were probably delighted too, when she took one glance around the hall and said, 'Leave us!'

Within seconds it was just her and I left.

'I distinctly remember telling you to avoid Cranock, not seek him out and try to get yourself killed.'

'I'm sorry, but I couldn't help myself. Throwing me out of my apartment was the last straw. I earned everything I have through sweat and blood and have come too far to be cast down into the slums again.'

'It's just an apartment.'

'Says she who lives in luxury as a God. Why don't you try living in some of the most basic accommodation that you so called Gods deemed us worthy of living in?'

Petra remained silent but drew me a look of scorn that said more than many words could.

'I'm sorry, I don't mean to aim my frustrations at you. It's just not in me to accept defeat or be pushed around by anyone. Particularly knowing what I now know. You should have let me fight him earlier.'

'If I had you would be dead.'

'Maybe, maybe not.'

'There's no maybe about it. Weaponless, as you were, you wouldn't have stood a chance. Only your ego is telling you otherwise.'

I looked away feigning insult but I knew she was right.

Petra came closer and placed her hand on my cheek, turning me to face her once again.

'Do you truly love me?'

'Of course,' I reply.

'Then please, do not go near Cranock again. Forget your ego and do as I say, just for now, until Cero decides who he will support. If he sides with us, then that should be the end of the matter.'

'And if he doesn't?'

'We worry about that later. For now, for me, can you promise you will remain here at camp and stay out of Cranock's way until the fight on Saturday?'

'I promise. I'll stay out the way this time.'

'Cranock has agreed to do the same at least until Saturday. I believe he will stick to that promise, with you defeating Cero's champ being of mutual benefit. Afterwards, he is not to be trusted. I will speak to Cero again and urge him to make a decision sooner than he planned. Hopefully on Saturday, when he and the other Gods arrive to watch the contest. Just make sure you win and don't let all this distraction affect you.'

'Don't worry, I'll win Saturday alright,' I reply confidently.

'Good. Now why don't you show me this lovely new accommodation of yours and we'll see if it's worthy of a Goddess staying over,' Petra says with a smouldering look.

Chapter 29

Good to my promise, I remained in the training camp the next two days, focussing solely on Saturdays contest. Even on Friday when the rest of the camp reported to the great pyramid to perform a welcoming display for the other Gods arriving, I remained on camp, despite being the star attraction and champion gladiator. However, it appears I was not missed or welcome either as no guards were sent to retrieve me, and when the camp's population returned that evening, not a single person mentioned a word of about my no show. Even the General was giving me a wide berth at the moment.

The evening before the fight proved to be long and lonely. Petra had informed me that she would not be visiting that night due to the arrival of the other Gods. She couldn't allow Cranock to have so much time alone with them, allowing him to scheme and plot against her or try to sway Cero's decision in his favour.

I also missed greatly the music and film collection I had in the apartment. Now back in basic accommodation, there was nothing to do but sit and stare at the walls. When I was on the rise through training camp, it never bothered me. Because I came from nothing, I was used to it. Having gained the luxuries in life that I did, it was hard going back the way now.

It certainly gave you plenty of time to think about things, which I did, over and over. Trying to imagine all the possible outcomes and angles of my current situation.

My mind eventually succumbed to sleep late into the night and I awoke early in the morning as a bright flash of red light filled the room. It was a welcome sight as Petra climbed into bed and lay beside me whilst describing the events of the previous evening. Not that there was anything significant to tell. Cero was apparently giving nothing away, whilst Dalip and Ti'ar showed no interest in listening to either side, but that was most likely pre-instructed.

The time for me to rise and ready, came and went with the comfort of Petra cuddled beside me too hard to leave. Finally, it is her who insists she must leave, but tells me she loves me and that she will return as soon as she can after the fight. We kiss one last time, before she wishes me luck, then disappears.

I sit for a moment, glancing around the small, basic accommodation as the silent, loneliness falls once more. I absorb it and promise myself, that this is not how my legacy ends. Not today!

I shower and get ready, expecting a knock on the door at any point as my lift to the arena arrives to collect me, but it never comes. I go out front and wait by the road for a while but still it does not arrive and finally I begin walking towards the main office building.

The receptionist there is extremely apologetic and asks me to take a seat whilst she tries to arrange transport. Twenty minutes later she tells me a car is on its way but it doesn't arrive for another thirty minutes. By the time we actually get underway, I'm over an hour by my scheduled time, but I try to not let it bother me. It's not by accident my car didn't arrive but if that is the level of games a so called God wishes to play, then so be it. It just makes him look even more foolish. The day was still young and my contest was not due to begin until early evening. I should still arrive at the arena around lunchtime which provides me more than adequate time to prepare.

The guard assigned to transport me looks a little nervous and doesn't say much, but I'm not in the mood for conversation anyway, so that suits me just fine.

Finally underway, we reach about the halfway point to the stadium, when I spot a cloud of dust rising in the distance as another vehicle speeds towards us. You rarely see many driving around, but on the day of a contest, vehicles driving to and from the arena is not unusual and so I never gave it a second thought. Not until I spotted the vehicle was a certain Mustang Shelby Gt500. My Mustang Shelby! Or at least it used to be.

Whoever was driving it certainly wasn't holding back, and flew by us so quickly I was unable to see the driver, not that I needed to. My old car, driving like a lunatic, it could only be one person and as I turned in my seat to watch it speed off into the distance, a wry smile formed on my face.

However, rather than watching the Mustang sail off into the sunset, the General hit the brakes hard and spun the car around, creating a huge circle of dust.

He immediately set off after us, flashing his lights and honking the horn as he approached.

'Pull over,' I instruct but the guard continued on driving as if not noticing the General behind us, which would have been damn near impossible. I instruct the guard to pull over once again, assuming he hadn't heard me the first time, but when he still doesn't pull the car over, I turn to face him and growl.

'I don't know what the fucks going on here, but you've got two seconds to pull this car over or I'm going to snap your neck and do it myself!'

The guard very quickly brought the car to a halt.

I was about to leap out the vehicle when something made me pause.

'Keys!' I demand holding my hand out.

The guard remained motionless, nerves and doubt etched all over his face. My patience was wearing thin however, and in the blink of an eye, my fist smashed into his jaw, which in turn sent his head crashing into the side window. The keys were handed over and I quickly got out the vehicle to find the General rushing around to meet me.

'I'm sorry son. I tried to get to you as quickly as I could, the minute I found out.'

'Found out what?' I ask beginning to feel nervous myself.

'Cranock's sent a hit squad to your parents' house.'

'What? To do what?'

'Kill them! To punish you for the other day.'

A wave of nausea fell over me instantly. I stupidly hadn't thought for a second that my actions would place my parents' lives in danger.

'Here, go!' snapped the General as held aloft the keys for the Mustang.

Without another word, I grabbed the keys and ran to the car. The engine roared to life once again and I sped off in a shower of dirt and sand.

It all made sense now. My transport not showing up wasn't just the silly game I thought Cranock was playing. It was a deliberate ploy to keep me from the arena and avoid any chance of me finding out what was transpiring with my parents. Even the guard that was driving me must have been in on it, no wonder he was nervous. He should be. He's a dead man the next time our paths cross. I had the Mustang going flat out and still it wasn't quick enough for me. I didn't know when the hit team had been sent, my parents could already be dead. The thought made my anger and nausea rise in equal measure.

It took around an hour to reach the area I was raised, but it felt like a day. I weaved through the tight streets like a man possessed until finally I turned into the row that included my parents' house.

My heart froze upon seeing an armed forces jeep parked outside their front door.

Screeching to a halt beside the empty jeep, I fear the worst. I was too late, I knew it. I'd thankfully avoided ever being involved in a hit squad but I knew enough about them to know that they generally didn't mess around. They went in and carried out the task they had been given, quickly and efficiently.

That sinking feeling of dread coursed through my veins as I climbed out the Mustang and ran towards the door. Yards away, I could see blood on the handle of the door, which lay slightly ajar. I pushed it open, wary of an oncoming attack. My entrance hadn't exactly been quiet and I was sure the guards would know who they were dealing with, which meant kill or be killed.

As the door swung open, no attack came, but the floor was soaked with blood and looked like bodies had been dragged across it, towards the rear of the house.

Voices!

I could hear voices coming from the rear of the house. Too preoccupied with their grisly task, it appeared my arrival had gone unnoticed. They would regret that. I crept through the door and began following the trail of blood, towards the voices. Anger threatened to boil over within me. Damn I was going to make those sons of bitches pay for what they just did.

'Jacob?'

I spin around instantly to see my mother sitting in the corner of the living room. She looks frail and shocked, but alive.

'Mom?' was all I could stutter, feeling shocked and confused myself. I'd been concentrating so much on the voices and the trail of blood I hadn't even noticed my mom in the corner of the room.

Before we could say anything else, footsteps from behind catch my attention and I spin around ready to attack.

'Whoa there son,' says my father, raising his hands.

'Dad! What's going on, are you okay?'

'It's okay son, we're fine. Come here.'

I relax my stance, stepping forward to hug my dad as relief floods through my body.

'Thanks to your friend,' he adds.

'My friend?'

'Ah, nice of you to finally join us,' announces another voice from behind my father.

I look up to see the old superior standing covered in blood and smiling.

'That God of ours, wants to be more careful who he chooses to be part of a hit squad.'

A large smile breaks out on my face now too. I rush towards the superior and throw my arm around him. 'Thank you, from the bottom of my heart.'

'Don't worry about it boy, figured you paid back the favour well last time so might as well get you in my pocket once again.'

'Anything you want is yours. Consider me in your debt for life for this.'

'Oh, I will. Unfortunately those lives might not last long once Cranock finds out about this, but what the heck. I was already dead inside until you brought me back to the forces again. If it happens now, at least I got to enjoy one last battle against Petra's army.'

'Well, I have an idea that, if successful might let you carry on a bit longer than you expect.'

'And if unsuccessful?'

'I'll definitely be dead and you lot won't be far behind me I'd imagine.'

'Do I even want to ask?'

'No, probably not,' I reply before setting off towards my mother. Tears filled her eyes, as I embraced her with a giant bear hug.

'Why did Cranock send a hit squad to murder the parents of his prized gladiator son?'

'Because he's an arsehole, Dad.'

My reply made the superior laugh, but my parents both grimaced with shock. Unaccustomed to hearing anyone speak so openly disrespectful about a God.

'That's the short version anyway. The longer one is complicated, but I will explain it all in time, just not right now. For now, I need to return to the arena urgently. I'm back in the basic accommodation, number 48. Can you take my parents there and watch them till I return?'

'Of course, consider it done,' replies the superior. 'Will it be safe enough there?'

I turn away from my parents and lower my voice. 'It should be for now, but if I don't return tonight………..' I pause trying to find the right words.

'It's okay, I understand,' says the superior, saving me from finishing the sentence.

'Thanks,' I reply gratefully, before turning to face my parents once again.

'I'm sorry to rush off, but I must go now if any of us are to stand a chance of surviving Cranock's wrath. The superior will take you to my house to wait for me and get you away from this bloodbath.'

'Where are you going, Son?' asks my father.

'To try and sort things out.'

'With Cranock? He is not a reasonable being, son. He will kill you. Please, stay with us,' my mom says pleadingly.

'It's the only way, I'm afraid. If I stay here, the only thing that will happen, is more guards will arrive to finish what the others have failed to do.'

My mom goes to say something further but I pull her towards me to hug and whisper, 'It's the only way Mom and I must go now. I love you.'

I then hug my father, before turning to leave the house, nodding to the superior on my way out.

The noise of the Mustang's engine fills the air as I put my foot to the floor on the accelerator and screech my way out of the street. Time to pick a fight with a God.

Chapter 30

It was late afternoon by the time I arrived back at the arena and my absence would have definitely been noticed by now, despite whatever efforts the General had taken to assist me. Approaching the first guard point, I fully expected to be stopped and held, not that I was going to comply but I expected them to try at least. However, that wasn't the case and I was allowed to enter the arena and make my way to the changing area as if nothing had happened at all.

Or maybe not quite. Rather than halting me in my tracks, it appeared to be the opposite. Everyone was giving me a wide berth as I strolled through the eerily quiets halls and corridors of an arena that currently held over one hundred thousand people.

It was fine with me if the guards wanted to give me a wide berth, but I was hoping to find the General. Unfortunately, he was nowhere to be seen.

My training and changing area were deserted, which allowed me to sit down and take a deep breath, as I tried to free my mind of the last few frantic hours and prepare for what lay ahead. Focussing and channelling my energy and anger.

Next, I changed into my combat clothing, which had at least been left in the changing area for me, along with my trusted swords, and made my way into the practise hall to stretch and prepare myself physically for the contest.

A short while later, the silence of the hall was broken when a door opened, then slammed shut as a guard entered to inform me that it was time to make my way to the sand.

I kept my eye out for any sign of the General on my route towards the entrance but still to no avail. Probably sitting with the dignitaries by now, I think to myself. Entering the tunnel that led to the sand, the noise level of the crowd above me rises dramatically, before turning suddenly to jeers and boos, signalling the arrival of my opponent into the arena.

'Good luck sir, should be a great contest,' says the guard who will signal my moment to enter.

Nodding thanks in reply, inside I laugh to myself thinking how it isn't going to be the show everyone was expecting.

'That's the green light, you're good to go sir,' announces the guard, before the large door before me suddenly shoots open and light streams into the dark corridor.

As I step out onto the sand for all the colosseum to see, a roar erupts from the crowd, cheering for their own champion. The noise was deafening and had it been under better circumstances, I would have taken my time to enjoy the moment and the crowd's adulation. Today however, it was straight down to business, marching purposefully towards the centre of the sand and my opponent.

Cero's champion watched me like a hawk, snarling menacingly, as I approached. His full and undivided attention centred on myself, whilst he was but a small afterthought to me now.

I reach the area where protocol would have me stop, around ten metres from my opponent. We would then normally turn to face the Gods, paying our respect and awaiting their signal to begin the contest.

Instead of stopping, I continue marching towards my opponent. Instinct makes his hand go towards the handle of his sword, surprised at my actions, but too well trained to be caught off guard so easily.

As he readies to draw his weapon, I change direction and begin marching towards the Gods. Even from their lofty position in the arena, I can see them casting strange looks towards Cranock, all apart from Petra. With a worried look upon her face, her eyes remained squarely on me.

I halt about twenty yards from the wall that circles the arena's sandy floor and continue to gaze towards the Gods, quickly scanning the area around them for any signs of the General, but sadly still finding none. The crowd had fallen silent, sensing something was afoot with my strange actions, and so I begin to address the arena.

'You have all come to see a battle of the champions today,' I bellow out as loudly as I can. 'Two prized fighters putting their lives on the line, as they have done many a time before, all at the request of their masters.'

I motion towards the Gods and see Cranock jump to his feet, looking furious. However, after the slightest of hand movements by Cero, he slowly sits back down again, allowing me to continue.

'I have fought for years under the guise of our God's so-called honour and victory motto and yet sadly I have found it is something he is very much lacking in himself.'

'YOU'RE DEAD GLADIATOR!' screams Cranock, rising to his feet again. This time Cero did likewise, placing a hand on Cranock's shoulder to halt him, before calmly saying,

'If you have a point to this very public display of disrespect, I suggest you get to it right now!'

'My point is this. Why should I fight for a God who demands honour above all else and yet just hours ago, sneakily sends a team of guards to kill my parents behind my back. Does that seem like an honourable way to treat a person that has served you so well, and given you so much in terms of honour and victory?'

Cero glances across at Cranock with a look that suggests I had called it right and Cranock's actions were his alone.

'I cannot serve such a God and if he has any honour at all in his veins then I call on him to accept the challenge I throw down and fight me here today, in the arena, one on one.'

A huge gasp of shock and murmur echoes around the arena upon hearing my words.

Suddenly a flash of red catches my eye from the Gods' area, before another one erupts much closer to me on the sand and Cranock appears, clearly fuming.

'I'll accept that challenge alright and I'll make you suffer in the process,' he spits out, as his large club like weapon begins to grow from his grasp.

I respond immediately by drawing both my swords, then surge forward to meet the oncoming Cranock. Two flashes of red light in the ground between us, signal the arrival of Petra and Cero onto the sand. Petra has her hand raised, motioning for me to stop. She is saying something too, but it is drowned out by a furious, loud, long scream by Cero.

'STOOOOOOOOOOOOOOOOOOOOOP………..'

It was so loud and ferocious, not only did Cranock and I halt, the entire arena froze. As Cero now looks from Cranock to myself, you could have heard a pin drop.

Red light flashes either side of me as Dalip and Ti'ar decide to join the party. Glancing over my shoulder at each of them, I can't say I was happy about the rather threatening position they have taken up around me. Unfortunately I wasn't in much of a position to do anything about it right now.

'How dare you both disrespect myself and the other Gods in this manner. I have brought my champion gladiator a long way to take part in what was supposed to be a special contest. One worthy of bringing all the Gods together and instead we find ourselves embroiled in what amounts to a petty dispute.'

At the mention of Cero's champion, everyone glances across to the centre of the sand where he stands alone, looking rather bewildered at the events unfolding before him.

'It seems you have forgotten your place in this world gladiator?' continues Cero, snapping my attention back to him.

'Having the gall to actually challenge a God! And disrespect all of us in the process? I should kill you myself right now.' As Cero's cold eyes stare at me in silence, as if deliberating whether to do just that, movement behind me, makes me turn to see both Ti'ar and Dalip, were now producing their weapons. This action then prompts Petra to draw her trusted golden daggers in a not so subtle manner and shoot Ti'ar and Dalip a look of warning.

'Perhaps the actions of others are somewhat to blame for your foolishness however,' says Cero, glancing at Petra.

A smirking Cranock, makes Cero turn around further and say, 'I'm not just referring to her. The gladiator is foolish and disrespectful but has a point at least.'

The smirk quickly disappears from Cranock's face.

'You gave me your word that no action would be taken against the gladiator until I had made my decision. I think killing his parents still falls into that bracket. Do you take me for a fool?'

Cranock doesn't respond immediately, instead staring at Cero with a menacing look that said that was exactly what he thought of their leader. Finally, he relents. 'Of course not. I simply felt it was my right as ruler of this land and this gladiator, to exert some kind of punishment for his behaviour. I did not realise our agreement extended beyond the gladiator himself.'

'Clearly,' replies Cero cynically. 'Our will is built upon honour, respect and taking responsibility for our own actions. We must do as we preach and therefore, I'm inclined to allow this fight to go ahead.'

'Good,' snarls Cranock, let's get on with it then.

Cero laughs lightly, before adding, 'A little patience Cranock. I said I will allow this fight to go ahead but it will not be today. Today was supposed to be about our two champions facing off against one another and I still intend on watching that spectacle before anything else happens.' Cero now turns to look at me. 'Prove you're worthy of this challenge that you throw down so willingly. Defeat my champion and you shall have your day of reckoning, one week from now. Agreed?'

'Fine with me, so long as my parents are left alone?'

'Cranock?'

'Fine,' replies a clearly annoyed Cranock.

'His parents too?' prompts Cero, unhappy at the clarity of Cranock's answer.

'I'll leave his parents alone too. At least until after the fight,' he adds with a smirk.

'Well gladiator, I imagine it's not just your own life you'll be fighting for next Saturday but you have my word no one will be harmed beforehand. Do you agree to the terms?'

'I do.' I wasn't exactly happy about essentially putting my parents' lives on the line, but it would be foolish to think they weren't already anyway.

'Alright, now that we've settled that, perhaps we can put our weapons away and enjoy the next contest?' Cero says, glancing at Petra, who in turn looks towards Ti'ar and Dalip for a moment before slowly retracting her daggers. The Gods on either side of me, follow suit before disappearing in a flash and returning to their lavish viewing area. Once they're gone, I sheath my swords. Cero gives Cranock a wry look as he was now the last one still holding a weapon.

'Fine,' he mutters, before it begins to retract into his hand and he disappears in another flash to join Ti'ar and Dalip. Petra looks towards me before disappearing too. Her face was hard to read and I can't decide whether she is angry with me or not. I'm sure I'll find out soon enough.

'Citizens of the New Earth.' Cero's voice now booms around the arena from the P.A. system.

'It seems we have reached a critical era for our New Earth. One where, the memories of your Gods arriving on this planet have become distant and forgotten. Many of you were not even born then, such as your champion gladiator here, and so perhaps this is part of the reason that he forgets his place in our world and feels no shame in disrespecting the Gods as he sees fit.

Such has his misguided confidence grown, he actually has the gall to throw down a challenge of combat to the very God that has rewarded him so well over the years.'

The murmurs and whispers of the crowd suddenly grew at this point as Cero pauses to allow his words to sink in and cast his unreadable gaze over me for a moment.

'His disrespectful actions are more than worthy of death and that is the price he will ultimately pay. However, I have decided to allow this challenge that he has thrown down to go ahead for one reason only. I think it will serve as a timely reminder to those of you who may have become confused as to your standing in our New Earth and as a way of showing who is firmly in charge of this world without having to cause any destruction on the scale of our arrival day.

This so called champion gladiator who stands before you, represents the best the human race has to offer. He is the strongest, fittest, and most skilled warrior among you and one week from today the world will see just how insignificant he is to us Gods.

Of course, that is all depending on whether your champion has the skills to defeat mine, before he even thinks about taking on a God. You all came here today, as did we, to see a battle between two gladiators and that will still go ahead. So if he's quite ready to continue with what he should have been doing today, we can begin?'

Cero looks towards me theatrically.

'I'm ready whenever you are,' I reply.

'Let us begin then!'

A huge cheer erupts around the stadium as Cero and I continue to stare at each other.

'Go earn your right to challenge a God, boy,' he commands for my earshot only, then disappears in a red flash.

For the first time today, my focus finally turned to the person it should have been on the first place. Cero's champion was slowly walking towards me, swords drawn, ready for action. I set off to meet him, striding purposefully, but keep my swords sheathed on my back for now. A year ago, less even, this would have been probably the biggest moment of my life. I'd have been desperate to put on a show to please the Gods and the crowd alike.

Right now however, it was just an inconvenience getting in the way of my ultimate goal, and so I aimed to treat it as such and also throw a middle finger salute back at Cero in the process. My own way of replying to his little speech there.

The noise of the crowd continued to rise as we drew closer to each other. Cero's champion had now increased his pace to match mine and the yards between us reduced drastically by the second until there was only ten yards of sand left to cover.

At this point I finally drew my swords from over my shoulders, spun them once in each hand, then threw them at my opponent with such speed and accuracy, he never stood a chance.

Both swords struck him on the centre of his chest, the tips exiting out of is back, with at least one of the swords ploughing through his heart in the process. The force knocked him clean off his feet and sent him sprawling backwards. By the time he landed on his back on the sand, he was already dead.

The arena fell into a stunned silence. It wasn't what they were expecting to see and it definitely wasn't the spectacle the Gods were expecting to enjoy. But that was my point. I knew the lack of entertainment would annoy them, as would the blatant show of disrespect from my following actions.

After clinching victory, a gladiator would always approach the Gods section of the colosseum and take a knee out of respect, before being congratulated and permitted to leave the arena.

Today I strode towards my opponent, placed one foot on his chest and pulled my swords free from his body. I then walked slowly towards the exit, without once looking back at the Gods or showing them any kind of respect at all. You could have cut the atmosphere in the arena with a knife and just imagining the looks I must have been receiving from the Gods made me smile inside.

Something made me suddenly decide to raise one of my swords in a one armed salute to the crowd. Initially, nothing happened, but a moment or two later a solitary voice rang out from somewhere in the arena.

Des-troy-er!

Des-troy-er!

Soon more and more voices began to join in with the chanting.

Des-troy-er!

Des-troy-er!

Before I knew it, the whole arena was cheering my name and now, it wasn't just me that was disrespecting the Gods. The crowd knew what I was doing and they were letting me know that they were on my side. The human race had finally just witnessed someone dare to stand up to the Gods.

Chapter 31

After disappearing down the tunnel, I presumed the Gods must have made a sharp exit from the colosseum as the crowd continued chanting my name and stomping their feet, which echoed loudly throughout the arena, even in the lowest reaches of building where my changing area was situated.

I don't think the crowd's support would have lasted as long if the Gods had still been in attendance and made me wonder whether I would be receiving a disgruntled visit from them shortly.

Instead of changing, I sat with my swords and combat clothing on for a while just in case, but thankfully it appeared that Cero might be staying good to his word and leaving me be until my contest with Cranock.

I finally showered and changed and set off to find the Mustang, managing to exit the arena without any interference and was soon on my way back to the training camp. A little doubt had begun to flicker through me, regarding my parents' safety on the journey home, but I gladly found them safe and well with the superior when I arrived at the accommodation.

As I recounted what had happened at the arena, my mom burst into tears upon hearing I had challenged Cranock to a fight, but mostly took the news relatively well. What else was there to say? I either took my chances against him or we all faced certain death now anyway.

We were all sitting in the small living room discussing the events of the day when a bright red flash engulfed the room and gave everyone, apart from myself, the fright of their lives. I was getting used it now.

I couldn't help but laugh at the look of shock on my parents and the superior's faces as they stared in disbelief at the sight of Petra standing before them. It got funnier yet as the realisation of who was before them sank in and they all began scrambling to get down on one knee, which in this tiny room meant their faces were almost banging off Petra's legs. Now even Petra looked a little taken aback at what was going on.

Unable to contain my laughter quietly anymore, it erupted loudly, which drew me a strange look from everyone.

'I'm sorry, I'm sorry, I couldn't help it.' I say still unable to contain my laughter fully.

'Get up Mom, Dad, it's okay.'

My parents throw Petra a cautious look first before moving.

'Please stand,' she urges them.

As my parents and the superior finally get to their feet I say, 'Petra, these are my parents. Mom, Dad, Petra and I are, well, in a relationship.'

My parents look at me as if I'm crazy for a second and now it was the superior's turn to have a wide grin on his face.

'Pleased to meet you,' says Petra.

'Oh, the pleasure is ours your highness,' replies my mom, doing an awkward looking curtsy.

'Perhaps I could have a moment alone with your son?'

'Yes of course,' answers my mom as she and my Dad look around wondering what to do.

'Come on, we'll go for a walk, I'll show you around the camp,' says the superior, still with a smile on his face.

'Thanks, I'll come and find you when we're done,' I say, seeing them out the door.

'Well that was an interesting day,' Petra says as I turn to face her.

'I'm sorry. I know it wasn't what you were expecting, but he left me no choice. He tried to kill my parents and would have succeeded had it not been for a stroke of good fortune in who was selected for the hit squad.'

'I'm not angry with you this time, just worried. I understand your actions, but I fear you may have taken on a battle beyond your abilities. I do not want to lose you,' says Petra placing her hand lovingly on my cheek.

'I don't want to lose you either and despite your lack of confidence, I don't intend to!'

'You know I don't mean it like that. I just know Cranock's full capabilities and God or not, he is a force to be reckoned with.'

'Perhaps, but you don't know what I'm fully capable of in the arena either.'

'True,' replies Petra, with a conceding the point look.

'Besides, the minute it came down to us and Cranock, it was inevitable it would come to a head at some point. Even if Cero came down on our side, you said yourself Cranock would not be able to accept it. At least this way the contest has been sanctioned by Cero and despite the fact he blatantly expects me to just lay down and die, if I do win then he will surely have no other choice than to leave us be.'

Petra frowns. 'I'm not so sure it will be as straightforward as that. You're only seeing it from the angle of you and me, but your actions earlier may have a much grander impact than you could imagine.'

'How so?'

'In the eyes of humans, you publicly disrespected not one, but all of the Gods and walked away without a care in the world. Even challenging a God to a fight in the process. Such behaviour has never been done since our arrival, such is our power and dominance over the planet. For humans to see one of their own act in such a way, may give them misguided hope that our rule over them is in decline. The planet's history tells us that many revolutions and uprisings have been sparked by incidents much smaller and trivial than those of today. Should you go on and defeat Cranock, it may lead to greater battles and conflict.'

'I'm sure any uprising or conflict brought on from my victory would be dealt with quickly and severely by Cero, considering the power he has to call upon up there,' I reply pointing towards the sky and their vessel that lies within the stars.

'That is true but the history of this planet and others, also shows us that once these kind of uprisings begin, they can be very hard to ever fully eradicate. Once your fear and dominance over something has been lost, it may never return.'

'I see,' I say sheepishly, causing Petra to laugh.

'That's not to say that's what's going to happen. It is one possibility from several outcomes, but we can worry about that later. For now, we must prepare you as best we can for the contest with Cranock. I will go now as I think I may be able to get you something that will help you in that manner, but I was hoping to return later. Will you all be staying here tonight?' asks Petra glancing around the tiny apartment.

This time I laugh. 'I'm pretty sure the next apartment is empty, I'll set my folks up in there with the superior and await your return.' I smile before taking Petra's hand and kissing the back of it.

She returns the smile, blows me a kiss, and then disappears.

The superior must have read my mind, for when he returns with my parents, he has already retrieved a key from the main office for the neighbouring apartment. Showing my parents into the accommodation, I face a barrage of questions regarding my relationship with Petra.

I can tell the superior is keen to ask some juicier questions but thankfully spares me the embarrassment in front of my parents. I'm sure I'll face them at some point however.

With my parents in the only bedroom and the superior taking the couch, I'm safe in the knowledge that should anyone try to enter the apartment, they will have to bypass him first.

Eventually returning to my own apartment, I settle on the small couch to await Petra's return, quickly becoming bored as I stare at the four walls and a blank screen. I miss the luxury of my previous accommodation, in particular, the many films I had come to love, but also the spectacular view I had, which I could sit and admire for hours at a time, listening to whatever music took my fancy.

I promised myself I would have it all back again soon and then some.

Suddenly the blank screen on the wall in front of me, burst into life. It was the first of no doubt, many, promotional videos for Saturday's contest. Didn't take them long to get that machine going. The video pretty much carried on from Cero's sentiments earlier, suggesting that it was he who had decided that the time had come to give the human race a reminder of their place on the New Earth. Very much playing down the fact that it was I who had challenged the Gods. It made out that it had been decided that they would take the greatest warrior of the humans and put him in the arena with Cranock to display just how weak and inferior, even the strongest human was compared to the Gods. A lot of shit is what it was, but sadly not a surprise. The video ended and returned the room to darkness. Staring at the walls, my eyes began to flicker before I dozed off into a light sleep. I'm not sure what time it was when the flash of red light awoke me again.

'See what you think of these,' Petra says offering me a long object wrapped in blankets.

I take the object from her and place it on the couch, quickly unwrapping the blankets to reveal two swords. I could tell right away that these were no ordinary swords however.

'At least with these you might stand a chance. They are made from a metal compound found on my home planet, far stronger than anything here on Earth. It is not quite the same as Cranock's weapon that has the ability to change its molecular structure, but as far as strength and density wise, it is more than a match.'

'Oh, that's okay, I don't need mine to grow and change shape, I prefer to know my weapons are solid. Thank you Petra,' I say before kissing her.

As we break apart, she says, 'Try them. They will feel heavier at first than your old swords, but at least you have the week to practice with them and get used to the feel.'

I pick up the two swords, weighing them in my grasp. They do feel heavier, but powerful and true at the same time which makes up for the extra weight. The metal has an almost blueish glow to it, similar to some of the other Gods weapons. There's barely enough room to swing a sword in the apartment, even without anyone else in it, so I head to the front door and step outside to give the swords whirl.

Petra watches from the doorstep as I go through the motions with them before, turning to face her with a broad smile on my face.

'I like them!'

'That's good, but you can practise tomorrow. Come back inside now,' she adds in her sultry voice, beckoning me with her finger. I immediately obey her command and follow her through to the bedroom, kicking shut the front door on my way.

Chapter 32

The following day I begin training with my new swords bright and early and quickly come to realise Petra had been right and I probably wouldn't have stood a chance against Cranock using my old swords. The new ones were cutting through Earth made swords like butter, as would Cranock's weapon have done to mine. It got to the point where I wasn't getting any decent sparring done and eventually had to give one of the new swords to my training partner. It wasn't ideal but better than nothing.

Later that day, when I met with Petra and explained my predicament, she said she would try to retrieve two more swords from their ship. True to her word, she returned to my apartment during the night with two more. They weren't quite crafted as nicely as my own, but Petra assured me they would be sturdy enough to withstand the rigours of my training sessions.

Now my training really got going and it was training partners I was going through rather than the swords. I took to my new weapons right away, which was another added bonus as a good fighter can fight with many weapons but to be at his true peak, he will be yielding the ones he is most comfortable with and favours above all else. Until receiving these new swords, I wouldn't have stepped into the arena through choice with anything but my trusted old swords.

The next few days rolled by smoothly enough, with training going well and Cranock seemingly keeping his promise to leave us alone at least until after the fight. My only growing concern was for the General. I hadn't seen or heard of him since he alerted me to the hit squad and gave me the keys to the mustang.

I checked in each day to see if he had returned to his office within the headquarters building at the training camp, but to no avail, and no one there had seen or heard from him either. I feared the worst for one of the very few people I had formed a genuine close bond with over the years. The path my life had taken was not one full of friendships. I could count my true friends easily on one hand, with just the General and the superior making the list. And that was fine, it's not something that bothered me, it's just the way it was.

This wasn't a world where people tended to turn up alive and well after they went missing, but still, I hoped for the best.

My parents had been insisting that they wanted to come to the arena to watch the contest live on Saturday. At first, I had been flat out against it, with the chances of me being killed high, I didn't want my parents to see their son die in what would no doubt be a very messy and painful manner, should Cranock have his way. Also, if I died on Saturday, they would be following after me very quickly. We all knew it. There was no point kidding on otherwise, but I felt if they were in the arena, they would be arrested immediately. At least if they were elsewhere they might have a chance to run and hide.

To where? Was their argument, and they had a point. There was nowhere to run and hide, not for any length of time, so what was the point really? They'd rather be there to see their son crowned victor over a God or follow him quickly into the next life.

The superior agreed with them of course and in the end, I couldn't really argue against their case. Petra was able to ensure they all had tickets allocated for the arena, so come Saturday, it truly was going to be all or nothing.

The night before the fight, I sat alone in the living room gathering my thoughts as the screen on the wall burst into life with yet another promotional video describing how unworthy I was and how much our dear, powerful God was going to teach me a lesson.

Something snapped within me, probably just sick of the sight of Cranock's smug face. I jumped up and ripped the screen right off the wall, before marching out the apartment and throwing the screen high into air. I watched as it landed on the hard tarmac, smashing into hundreds of pieces. It was childish, but it brought a smile to my face.

An ordinary citizen could be killed for such an act, but what were they going to do to me now?

I jumped a little as another screen came out of nowhere and smashed off the tarmac. Laughing at myself, I turned around to see the superior and my parents standing nearby.

'They were getting on our nerves too,' said my father with a smile. 'You'll show em who's the real champ tomorrow son.'

'Thanks Dad.' For their sake, I hope he's right.

'You want to come in and join us? Or is your fancy lady coming by tonight?'

My dad's description of Petra made me laugh once more and it felt good.

'Yes Dad, she'll be round at some point, but it's okay, you go in, it's getting late. I'm just going to watch the stars for a while and relax my mind.'

'You sure son?' asked my Mom.

'Positive, in you go. Don't worry we'll have plenty of time tomorrow before we need to leave for the arena. Try and get some rest, big day ahead,' I reply before kissing my mom on the forehead.

'It's you who should be resting,' she protests, but I wave her off.

'Don't worry I'll be rested and ready come tomorrow. In you go, I'll see you in the morning.'

As my parents and the superior finally relented and retired for the night, I wandered over to the Mustang and lay back on its hood. It was a clear night and the sky offered up a spectacular view of the stars and distant galaxies. I stare at them in awe, and wonder about all the other inhabited planets that Petra spoke of.

After a while, a voice calls out from my open doorway.

'Stargazing are we?'

I sit up to see Petra standing at the doorway.

'Yeah, come here, join me.'

Petra wanders over slowly and gives me a look that says, 'I'm not lying down on that.'

'Come on lie down, enjoy the view. You can tell me what I'm looking at.'

Again the look.

'What? Is it beneath a God to lie on a classic Mustang with such a lowly being?' I jest.

'Perhaps,' she replies.

'Aw come on, it might be the last chance either of us gets to do it.'

Petra shakes her head and sighs before finally climbing onto the hood and laying down beside me.

'The view is good, I'll give you that,' she says. 'Not so keen on the comfort factor.'

I put my arm around her and pull her close to me. 'Better?'

'A little.'

'Show me what's out there. Which direction is your original home?'

'Somewhere far, far away in that direction,' replies Petra, pointing to the sky.

'Do you miss it?'

'No not really. At least not now. I did at first when our mission was in its early days but it has been so long now, it has become more of a distant memory, or feels like a previous life.'

'If you could, would you go back?'

'Well that isn't possible so the question is redundant.'

'Everything's impossible until it isn't, so just pretend that it is, would you return?'

Petra went silent as she mulled over the question for a moment.

'Only if you came with me. Would you?' she eventually replied, turning the question back on myself.

'Hell yes!'

She smiled, 'Good answer. Now can we go inside and lie down on something more comfortable?'

'Alright, alright, come on then.'

Chapter 33

The following morning, after waking, Petra and I, lay cuddled together for a long time, quietly enjoying each other's warmth and touch. Neither of us said it, but we both knew it might be the last time we ever did so and therefore, took our time enjoying each and every minute of it.

Only when the time dictated it was necessary to get out of bed and get ready, did we do so. As much as Petra had opened up during our relationship, she was still a cold and calculated person at heart, capable of mass murder. So it was no surprise really that she didn't do farewells very easily. But then, neither did I, so we were suited well on that front.

Upon parting company, she said she loved me and that if I didn't win, she would kill me herself. What can you say to that?

I then spent some time with my parents, before a slightly more tearful farewell with them. A vehicle had been arranged to take them to the colosseum along with the superior, who wished me good luck before leaving for the arena. My parents had asked me to travel with them, but I opted to go solo. One last drive in the Mustang was just the thing needed to get you in the right frame of mind and so, once everyone else was long gone, I packed my gear, then put my foot to the floor and sped off at break neck speed.

The drive was exhilarating and made me think about the General more, remembering the many fun races we'd had in various vehicles. I was almost disappointed when the drive ended and I reached the arena. I passed through the guard points, parked up the mustang and made my way towards the changing area. Anyone I met, was acting cagey around me, which I could understand. The word was out, that any support shown for myself would be looked down upon.

The propaganda videos that had been showing all week had made that abundantly clear. Support your God, show your loyalty or pay the price had been the gist of it. And so you could understand why folk were fearful of showing me any support.

Entering my dressing room, I changed into my combat gear straight away, keen to get warmed up in the training hall. The large training area was deserted, which suited me just fine. As I began going through the motions, I noticed a box lying in the centre of the room. Nothing unusual looking about it other than the place it had been left. I presumed someone would be returning to collect whatever was inside and never gave it a second thought until my routine took me close by it and a sudden dose of curiosity got the better of me.

Pausing to stare down at the box, I noticed the lid of it had been slid open ever so slightly. Something about it looked deliberate, off even. I stretched out with one of my swords and flicked the lid off completely.

Fuck!

Staring back up at me was the General's decapitated head. I say staring, but his eyes had been crudely removed, leaving two bloody, dark gaping holes.

I didn't know what had happened since I last saw the General, but it sure looked like he'd suffered, if his head was anything to go by, and I damn sure knew who was to blame.

'Sorry sir, you didn't deserve to die like this. I promise you, I'll give it my all to make sure he pays for his actions,' I say before kneeling down to replace the lid over the box.

I definitely wasn't lacking in motivation for the fight already, but Cranock had just added yet more fuel to the fire burning inside me.

Springing to my feet, I get to work on my warm up routine with renewed vigour. Once finished with that, I sit in the silence of the vast hall, gathering my thoughts until finally a door springs open and a guard shouts in, 'Time to make your way to the sand, sir.'

I pick up my swords and begin to make my way up to the arena. Normally I'd sheath my weapons on my back until the fight began, but the new swords were slightly larger and didn't fit my old sheath, so it was left behind today.

Entering the final tunnel that led to the sand, a huge cheer erupted from the stands above me, meaning Cranock had just made his entrance. It was loud, very loud and yet lacked the true sound from a roar of passion. It sounded exactly what it was. A cheer of fear. A noise made from instruction, rather than passion and true support.

A curt nod was exchanged with the guard upon reaching the sand entrance. Several smaller cheers continued to arise as Cranock no doubt was part milking, part mocking the crowd.

I inhaled deeply through my nose, as the scents of years of blood, sweat and sand drifted towards me. If this was to be my final contest I would truly miss it. I loved being a gladiator. A champion. A warrior. I wondered what would have become of my life if the old superior hadn't spotted me all those years ago. Something made me believe I would have found another way here had he not. I was born to fight. This was my calling in life.

The guard mumbled something but I wasn't listening. A second or two later the door shot up and bright light streamed into the dark tunnel. I shut my eyes and smiled, allowing the light to embrace me for a moment.

Time to do what I did best!

Chapter 34

For the first ever time, I walked onto the sand to the sound of silence. It didn't come as a surprise however. The message to the masses on who to support had been crystal clear all week. I wasn't fazed, it was just different from what I was used to. I could see Cranock standing in the centre of the sand, grinning broadly with immense satisfaction at my silent entrance. Such was his ego, he probably believed this was the crowd's true feelings.

Pausing for a moment, I turn to face the stands to search for my parents and the superior, scanning the crowd until I find them gazing down at me. I raise one of my swords, touching my heart first before holding it aloft in a little salute to them. I'm about to lower it when I decide to continue my salute to the whole arena. It wasn't a pre-planned action, just something I took the notion to do. The crowd had supported me like a champion, long before I was one. From my very first battle at the tender age of sixteen, so it was just my little show of appreciation towards them for that.

I spin around slowly with a solitary sword held high in the air, until reaching my parents section once again. My mom looked like she was crying and my dad placed his hand over his heart in his own little salute back at me. Just then, I noticed a man close to them raise a solitary arm in the air. I wondered what he was doing for a second before noticing another man close by do the same, followed by the woman next to him. Suddenly it was spreading like wild fire, as solitary arms were being raised all around the arena in what I now realised was their own salute of support back at me. It was quite a sight to behold as the entire arena, bar the Gods now stood with one arm raised in the air.

A cheer, silent in action but deafening with meaning.

Turning back to face Cranock, I march towards him with purpose, noticing the broad smile has been wiped from his face. As I neared, his gaze was drawn to my weapons.

'Nice swords. Wonder where you got them from,' he says, glancing in Petra's direction.

'You seem worried?'

'Of you? Ha, I think not. Outraged, perhaps, that a lowly piece of scum like you has the gall to stand before me like this. I could end your life in a heartbeat, but I'm not going to let you off the hook so easily. This will be bloody, slow and extremely painful.'

'Yeah, yeah, so you keep saying old man!'

Cranock bristled with annoyance and fury at my continued disrespect, which in turn pleased me greatly. Any further chat between us was cut off by Cero's loud voice booming around the arena.

'Citizens of the New Earth, the time has arrived for you to witness how the very best you have to offer, the champion of humans, fares when he dares to challenge a God.

With no introductions required on this special occasion, let the slaughter commence!'

Cranock and I stood facing one another, with neither of us willing to take our eye off each other during Cero's short speech.

A blue glow suddenly extended from Cranock's right hand as his club-like weapon began to grow from his grasp. Readying to engage, I noticed a glint of silver as a small piece of metal now appeared in his left hand. It too began to grow and grow, on and on until I suddenly realise what it is.

A menacing grin flashes across Cranock's face before he says, 'Not the only one that can borrow weapons!'

The weapon Cranock held in his left hand was one of Dalip's feared and extremely deadly whips. I foolishly opened my mouth to respond when I should have been fully concentrating on his movement and actions. A quick flick of his left wrist sent Dalip's whip hurtling towards me. I threw myself backwards and to the left just in time to avoid a more serious hit, with the very end of the whip just catching my right shoulder. A graze from the whip was still enough to slice through my clothing and open up a sizable cut on my skin. Thankfully it wasn't deep and wouldn't hamper my own actions, at least not yet.

Cranock sent the whip hurtling back at me immediately but I managed to dive to my right and avoid any contact at all this time. In the blink of an eye it was surging towards me once more, this time I managed to bat it away with one of my swords. The impact as the two weapons collided sent a shower of blue sparks into the air. The next few minutes consisted of Cranock tormenting me with Dalip's whip, as I batted off the weapon or ducked and dived across the sand, trying to avoid being sliced open.

Wondering how I was ever going to get around the nuisance of a weapon, it suddenly began to detract and slide backwards into itself again until it was nothing more than a small stick in Cranock's hand. He must have become bored toying with me and decided he wanted some closer up action as he suddenly sped across the sand so quickly it was just a blur of movement and I only just realise in time that his large club was swinging towards my head.

Ducking sharply to avoid the weapon, I'm oblivious to his left fist following up, until it connects flush on my chin. The blow shakes me to my boots and sends me tumbling to the sand. I recover just in time to move out the way of the oncoming bat, before receiving a kick to the midriff that sends me hurtling through the air. Upon landing, I spring to my feet in time to finally swing an attack of my own. Unfortunately, Cranock meets my swinging sword head on with his club, which collides with such force, the impact knocks my sword free from my grasp, nearly breaking my hand in the process.

A stamp kick sends me backwards, colliding into the wall of the arena and knocking my other sword from my grip. I scramble across the sand to collect it, but inches from my reach, I have to dive back again to avoid Cranock's club.

I need a weapon and waste no time in setting off across the sand to collect the first sword I dropped. Yards away, something suddenly wraps around my right leg, then yanks me to the ground. It was no surprise to find the silver of Dalip's whip wrapped tightly around my leg and before I have the chance to try and free myself, I notice Cranock standing with his arm outstretched ready to yank hard on the whip.

Shit!

In an instant I find myself being dragged painfully across the arena floor before slamming into the surrounding wall once again. Above it all, the only sound that I can hear coming from the entire colosseum is Cranock's laughter. I somehow have to change the flow of this contest before it's too late. Another tug on my leg and I'm sliding back across the sand, face down.

Managing to push myself over onto my back, I sit up just enough to spot what I'm looking for. Out of reach for now, I have to take another couple of painful journeys across the arena floor, scrambling in the direction required in between. The next time I'm ready, and concentrate on the sword as hard as I can in between bits of sand and dirt flying into my face. A glint of blueish silver passes by and I thrust out my arm, hopefully.

Rolling to a stop, I quickly spin around and chop down with the sword in my grasp, snapping clean through the silver whip, producing another shower of sparks in the process. A huge cheer suddenly rises up from the crowd and the remaining thread of whip that was attached around my leg, thankfully loosens off, allowing me to free myself of it.

Rising to my feet I'm surprised to find Cranock still laughing.

'Listen to all these fools cheering, merely because you managed to temporarily free yourself from my weapon,' he shouts.

'Temporarily?' was my first thought. Glancing towards the damaged whip, I notice it has already begun repairing itself, growing back to its original length.

A second or two later it comes flying towards me, cracking mid-air in the spot I just dived away from. I need to get rid of that weapon once and for all and to do that I will need to shift myself as fast as I possibly can.

I pace slowly from side to side, as Cranock lines up for another crack of the whip. I want to appear to be an easy target without actually being so. He draws his left arm back, then as soon as he yanks it forward, I dive into a forward roll. The whip cracks harmlessly behind me as I emerge from my roll onto my feet, surging forward to make up the ground between us before he can re-load and strike at me at will.

I put everything I have into the short sprint towards Cranock and boy do I move fast. I move so fast I become a blur. Just like them! It's almost too fast for me to handle, but thankfully, I keep my control well enough to know when to duck so as to avoid Cranock's swinging club. As it arcs toward my head, I dive to his left, into another forward roll, swinging my own weapon, hopefully, at the right point. My forward momentum takes me beyond the reach of another counter attack by Cranock, before coming to a halt. A sharp draw of breath could be heard around the arena before a huge cheer erupts from the galleries.

I spin around to find Cranock stumbling across the sand, staring in shock at his handless arm. My gaze quickly scans the sand until I find Dalip's whip, which has shrunk into a little metal rod and lies harmlessly on the ground next to Cranock's severed hand.

The crowd's wild cheering suddenly begins to die and as I turn my attention back to Cranock I can see why. Their belief that I had just gained a major advantage in the fight was now being overshadowed by a rather, well, God like act.

Cranock had quickly overcome his shock and now stood in the centre of the arena with his severed arm raised aloft. However, rather than blood continuing to stream from the end of it, it had begun to heal and regrow at a frantic pace.

To almost all the watching crowd in the arena and millions more watching it on screens across the globe, it was a miracle, capable only by a God. To myself and the other Gods it was a demonstration of supremely advanced technology working as it was designed to, but certainly no miracle. Petra had explained to me one night how the super chip implanted in their heads gives them the ability to heal instantly. It's not that they heal much differently from ourselves, it's just speeded up to an instantaneous process. That was the simplified version anyway, but unfortunately I wasn't exactly in a position to explain that to the watching world right now.

At least I had managed my aim of freeing Cranock of Dalip's whip and whilst he was now busy stretching out his newly formed hand, I advanced.

Without raising his head he asks matter of factly. 'How did you do that?'

'Do what?' I reply, cautious not to be caught off guard whilst he speaks again.

'Move like that? What has she been giving you?'

'She's not been giving me anything other than the swords. You're just getting old?'

'No, that's not it. You moved quicker than is possible for a normal human being.'

I laugh, unsure how to respond. Was he just trying to mess with my mind? Don't let him in, focus. Keen not to engage in any kind of trash talking, I surge forward and attack. My sword clashes against his club with an almighty clang and the impact shudders through my arm. Again I attack, again he blocks. He blocks several more attacks, then as our weapons clash again, I quickly swing my free left fist around, which smashes right into his jaw and draws the crowd into life once more.

Cranock stumbles off to the side, before spitting a gob of blood onto the sand.

'Like that you little shit?' he growls. 'You shouldn't be able to match me. She's given you something, I know it. Tell me, I demand to know?'

'You demand?' I snort. 'Where do you think you are old man? Take a look around, the time of you demanding me to do anything is over, stop looking for excuses. Perhaps evolution has finally caught up with the false Gods?'

My comments enrage Cranock as he roars with anger before leaping forward to attack with renewed vigour. It's my turn to stumble backwards now as the force of his club pounding against my sword becomes unbearable. Unable to keep the sword in my grasp any longer, a final swinging blow knocks it free and sends it flying halfway across the arena.

I now duck and dive for survival, taking odd kicks and punches along the way as I once again fight to level the advantage.

Gaining his confidence back, Cranock takes a particularly wild swing, missing and over extending himself. I don't need any encouragement to take advantage. I step forward and send a crushing forehead straight into his face, then throw the arm holding his club over my shoulder and heave down on it with all my might. Bones snap, Cranock screams, and his trusted club falls to the floor.

As I release his arm, he scrambles away from me and any immediate further injuries. I bend over and pick up his fabled club, finding, as expected, it is much heavier than my swords, but still easy enough to control. I turn to face Cranock with a smile on my face, taking practise swings with his club. However, he is too busy with his own task in hand to pay attention to my gloating.

He gulps in several large gasps of air then pulls his broken arm back into alignment to allow the healing to begin.

The noise is sickening and makes the crowd gasp in shock. Cranock looks ready to be sick for a minute himself and yet moments later, their super fancy technology has done the trick again and he is busy flexing the mended arm.

'Neat trick,' I call out. 'But you and I know that's all it is,' I add, tapping a finger off my head. 'Once I take your head away from you, there will be no miracle growing that back.'

'Easy to talk like that when your opponent is unarmed and at a disadvantage,' replies Cranock, making me laugh.

'It didn't seem to bother you a minute ago!'

'So, tell me, who is your mother, your real mother?' asks Cranock in a surprising change of subject.

'What?' I stammer, thrown a little by the strange question.

'You heard me. Who is you mother?'

I pause, staring at Cranock as I try to decide where he is going with his head games.

'I'm sure you know who my mother is, you did try to kill her after all.'

'Her I know, but I think we both know by now, that is either not your true mother or she has been living for a long time under a false alias. Or are you so foolish, you still cannot see what is in front of you?'

Cranock begins to laugh, upon seeing the uncertainty over my face.

'I shouldn't laugh, for I am just as foolish not to have noticed it before now. I could always see you were supremely skilled for a human, it seems we just didn't push you hard enough to bring out your full potential, otherwise we would have known long before now and could very well have avoided all this unnecessary ill feeling between us.'

I knew exactly what Cranock was eluding to and yet still I couldn't quite fathom the idea as I stood dumbstruck in the middle of the arena.

'It will be interesting to see what, if anything, springs from the labours of your relationship with Petra. For when we first arrived on this planet, it became abundantly clear that a child would be impossible to bear from our mixed species. The difference between our genetic make-up appeared to be too great. That's not to say pregnancies did not occur, they did from time to time, but they would never last long and usually ended in the death of both mother and child. On rare occasions the mother survived, but was left well beyond any hope of future offspring.

Impossible, or so we thought. It appears evolution has evolved and we must conclude that in actual fact, we stand here today, fighting one another as father and son!'

I knew the reference was coming, but actually hearing it aloud made my head spin. This couldn't be true, but memories flashed through my head of how easily I had destroyed opponents. I was always head and shoulders above anyone else. Even now, I knew I had the beating of Cranock and yet I shouldn't have. They were too fast and too strong for humans, but not me. I was faster and stronger. As much as I wanted him to be lying, it did make sense.

Rumours of Cranock's liking for beautiful young human females was notorious and there was always at least five – ten of them, staying in luxury quarters high in the great pyramid. The turnover was high and frequent and when they left, most were never seen again.

Was I really Cranock's son? The thought repulsed me and yet I couldn't deny it was a possibility. I glanced to where my parents were in the stands. I needed to speak to my mom and find out the truth.

'We shouldn't be fighting each other, we should be ruling together. You my son, by my side!' said Cranock as he began to walk slowly closer.

All I could do was shake my head in disbelief.

'Lower your weapon and let us show the crowd we are one. We can rule over this land together, father and son.'

Cranock now stood before me, open handed, willing me to accept his offer.

'If you are my father, then what became of my mother? Did she die or is that truly her, up there in the galleries?'

'Who knows? There have been so many, who really cares about some human female whore? She means nothing, but you, you have God's blood running through your veins.' Cranock reached out and placed one hand on my shoulder. 'We are alike!'

I slowly shake my head once more. 'We are not alike. You talk about honour and loyalty, yet show neither. Even if it is true that you are my father, I could never stand by your side. I despise you!'

A crude smile appears on Cranock's face.

'At least you're honest boy, I'll give you that. And if it's honesty you want then I'll give you some. I'd never let an unwanted mongrel half breed like you anywhere near my throne.'

Cranock's hand on my shoulder grips down tight, before a flash of silver catches my eye from his free hand as a small blade suddenly appears in it and is thrust towards my heart.

I drop Cranock's club in my rush to knock his hand off my shoulder, allowing me to move backwards away from the incoming blade.

Just not quickly enough.

Pain erupts in my left shoulder as Cranock's blade strikes my body, but it could have been much worse. The instinctive movement of twisting my left shoulder inwards to protect the heart has saved my life, making the blade miss its true target. As I stumbled backwards, Cranock bends over to retrieve his club, which allows me a moment to recover my composure before he launches another attack.

In need of a weapon, I turn to the nearest one to me and grip the handle of the small dagger that is protruding from my shoulder. Gritting my teeth, I pull it free and ready myself for the oncoming Cranock.

He swings his club wildly and ferociously as if sensing he has me all but beaten, when in fact he couldn't have been more wrong. The advantage of a misguided sense of superiority he once had over me was gone. For several decades he has lived an easy life of luxury, whilst I have been training and fighting nearly every day. With no speed, strength or phycological advantage over me, it was now like an ordinary citizen versus a champion gladiator.

Each time I duck or sidestep one of his wild swings, I step in close and do a little damage with the dagger. Slicing open his abdomen and thighs with ease as I deliberately toy with him. With each cut, Cranock's rage grows and in turn his own attacks become wilder and desperate.

As much as I'm enjoying inflicting these wounds, they were sadly healing just as quickly. To actually end this fight once and for all, I knew I needed to inflict the kind of damage he would not be able come back from.

Cranock aimed another swing at my head, which I ducked easily, then grabbed his arm and sent the dagger stabbing into it, just before the elbow joint. Effectively disabling his arm for the time-being and causing him to drop his weapon.

I left the dagger in there this time, and followed the move up with a quick head butt, forcing Cranock to stumble backwards. I advance immediately and send a crushing punch right into the centre of his chest. This time the impact sends him sprawling onto the sand.

As he struggles to sit up and remove the dagger that is still embedded in his arm, I grab hold of his head and began to rain down a flurry of punches upon him until his face is a bloodied pulp. I then spin around to the rear, keeping him in the seated position with one arm squeezing tightly around his neck.

Looking towards the stands, our position was perfect. Directly in front of the Gods section. I glance up, catching Cero's rather stunned looking gaze, before I begin applying immense pressure to Cranock's neck, twisting and squeezing it as hard as I can.

He begins to make horrible noises, as blood and spit bubble from his mouth and nose.

'This is from the General!' I whisper into his ear, moments before a sickeningly loud crack signals his neck has finally broken.

A strange silence falls over the arena. Not the kind of noise that normally greets the end of one of my victories but an understandable one. Perhaps shock at what they had just witnessed, or uncertainty at whether or not Cranock could pull off another miracle recovery. Whatever the reason, it made for an eerie atmosphere as I walk across the sand to collect one of my swords, before making my way back towards the stricken figure of Cranock.

I reckoned even with his fancy healing technology, a broken neck was not something he would be able to recover from, at least not by himself, but I wasn't for taking any chances. Also, there was something I required from him too.

Upon reaching the fallen God, I bend over and heave his limp body up into a seated position, then grab a fist full of his hair to hold him in place and raise my sword, ready to strike.

I pause to look towards Cero once again, his cold eyes staring intently back at me.

In the blink of an eye, I bring my sword down and slice through Cranock's neck, chopping his head clean off his shoulders.

He definitely wasn't coming back from this one and the crowd knew it too as the arena finally erupted in triumphant noise. Not quite ready to join in with them just yet, I keep my gaze on Cero who has risen to his feet, followed closely by the other Gods.

I then raise my arm and hold Cranock's head aloft in a show of celebration and also a little, 'Fuck you!' at Cero for all his derogatory talk about me before the contest. Probably not the best idea to immediately start taunting them, but I was in full battle mode. I had just beaten a so called God that no one thought I was capable of doing and feel on top of the world. If Cero and the others wanted to come down to the sand and settle this right now, I was game, for sure.

However, without even the slightest change of expression, Cero merely disappeared in a flash of red light. As did Ti'ar and Dalip. Only Petra remained. As my eyes fall upon her beauty, all the rage coursing through my veins begins to ease and a large grin forms on my face.

My look was reciprocated as Petra smiles subtly back at me, nodding her head slightly to say well done before she too, disappears in a flash of red light.

I raise both arms, holding my sword and Cranock's head aloft in a victory salute, joining in with the crowd's wild celebrations.

Chapter 35

I now sat alone in my changing room as the noise of the jubilant crowd still rings out from above. The adrenaline of the fight was beginning to wain and my thoughts were turning to the revelations I had discovered during it. Did I have God's, or false God's blood running through my veins, whichever way you wanted to look at it?

The speed in which I moved during the contest was undeniably, God-like. Judging by Cranock, my strength couldn't have been too bad either, but how was this even possible? I needed to speak to my parents, who themselves were probably thinking the same thing, for ten minutes later a guard knocks on the door before sticking his head in.

'Sorry to bother you sir, but there's a superior officer and a couple that claim to be your parents, trying to get access to see you.'

'Its fine, let them through please.'

'Yes sir, will do,' replied the guard before exiting the room. Several minutes later, the door knocks once again before my parents enter, followed by the superior.

My mother was in tears and even my father seemed close to them as we embrace and enjoy the moment.

'That was incredible! How did you manage to move like them?' asks a jubilant superior, without thinking too much about what he was asking.

I look at him then glance towards my mom. 'That's something I need to find out for sure myself.'

The superior didn't take long to click. 'Ah, oh right, I see. Maybe I'll step outside and give you all some privacy to talk.'

'Thanks,' I reply, nodding my appreciation.

Once the superior had left the room, I turn to face my mom. Her tears of joy and relief, have now turned to ones of distress and worry. I place a hand on her shoulder. 'Don't worry Mom, nothing will change the fact that I love you both and as far as I'm concerned, you will always be my true mom and dad. But I need to know the truth, that's all I ask of you.'

My mom wipes away her tears and nods.

'Please don't hate us for not telling you. It just.............well, I guess it was just easier and safer not to, and we could never have predicted things would play out the way they have.

But as I suspect you now know, Cranock was your biological father.'

I look at my father but his eyes have averted towards the floor. Before I can say something, my mother continues.

'It was in the early years of the Gods arriving when I was still young and relatively pretty. I was working one day when some guards appeared and started examining all the females. Eventually they came over to me and told me I was being re-assigned and was to go with them immediately. It was worrying and strange, but what could I do? If a guard tells you to do something you do it and so I was put in the back of a vehicle and driven away from the settlement that had been my home since birth, never to return or see my parents again.

From there, we drove to several neighbouring settlements until three more girls had joined me in the vehicle. We were then taken on a long journey, eventually arriving at the great pyramid. Although we were confused and scared, there was also a sense of excitement initially as we were being told we were special and lucky to have been chosen to perform a very personal duty for our God. However, we soon learned that special duty was anything but, and we had instead become nothing more than a play thing for Cranock when he so desired.

He would use and abuse the many girls that lived out of sight in the upper echelons of the great pyramid until he either became bored with them or impregnated them. Both of which, usually had the same end result.

Girls would disappear regularly, never to be seen again. As for the ones who became pregnant, it was clear from the start that our two species did not mix well, biologically speaking, but he kept those around who fell pregnant, perhaps he wanted a child or maybe it was just down to curiosity, who knows? Whatever the reason, they remained and suffered agonising pain and sickness, ranging from weeks to months, with most eventually succumbing to death.

Only once did I ever witness one of the girls lasting right through to the birth, before dying whilst delivering a stillborn.

Had I remained in the pyramid during my pregnancy, I doubt I would be here today. As it was, luck was on my side, for when I was in the early days of my pregnancy, so early I was unaware of it yet myself, Cranock must have decided he'd had enough of me and I was to be cast aside.

Without warning, a guard arrived one day and instructed myself and another girl to follow him. We were then loaded into the back of a vehicle and driven a great distance from the pyramid. Only when we finally stopped beside an old mining quarry, did we realise what was happening. The guard ordered us out of the vehicle and marched us towards the edge of the quarry. It was huge and no way of surviving the long drop to the water and rocks below.

At least now we knew what happened to all the other girls that disappeared. It made sense I guess. There was no way an egotistical God who preached on about honour and loyalty would want to run the risk of having witnesses running around describing the dark sadistic truth about our so called wondrous God.

The guard drew his sword and told us we could either jump of our own accord or die the hard way, then be thrown over the edge. I was too much in shock to say anything but the girl with me was a fiery one and immediately began berating the young guard, who already appeared uncomfortable with the situation himself. Keen to gain control again, he began to shout back at the girl, threatening her with his sword, but rather than back down, his actions only further enraged her. The girl lunged forward, clawing at the guard's face with her nails.

The guard screamed in pain and anger, throwing the girl off him before launching a frenzied attack of his own, thrusting his sword in and out of the poor girl, repeatedly over and over. Eventually the young guard relented, staggering backwards as he looked down in shock at what he had just done.

'Why didn't she just jump? What have I done?' he began saying to himself over and over.

As if suddenly just remembering I was standing there too, he went quiet again, turning to face me. I was so terrified I couldn't do a thing. I was frozen to the spot, waiting to be brutally slaughtered as the other girl had been.

But the guard never attacked or said another word, instead he dropped his sword, stumbled back to the vehicle and took off, leaving me standing alone in the middle of nowhere, next to the bloody remains of the other girl.

Fearful the guard would get over his shock and return to finish the task he had been ordered to do, I began to run as fast as I could away from the quarry. Initially, I thought I had been lucky to have been spared but that feeling quickly vanished, when I spent the next three days and bitter cold nights, alone and lost in the desert. With no food, barely any water and ill-equipped clothing for the harsh conditions, it was beginning to feel like jumping into the quarry would have been the better option after all.

On the fourth night and close to death, I finally stumbled upon a settlement. Too exhausted and cold to care about guard patrols or otherwise, I started banging on doors, begging for someone to help me, but no one did. At least not until I reached your father's house. He was the only person who had even opened their door and thankfully when he saw the sorry state of me sitting on his doorstep, didn't hesitate to help, despite knowing full well the kind of trouble he could find himself in.

As it was, fortune seemed to be on our side and no guards came knocking on the door over the coming days and weeks as your father nursed me back to health and I confided in him all that had happened to me.

Our next problem however, was how to get me back into society without raising any alarms, which was easier said than done. Your father had a brother who was in the armed forces and he managed to get word to him that he needed help. The brother arrived at the house one evening to find out what the issue was, which led to a long and heated argument between him and your father. It was understandable. What we were asking of him would be a death sentence for all of us if discovered. Thankfully he was a good man at heart, just like your father and when he eventually left the house that evening, he promised he would try his best to assist us.

Another week or so passed, before he returned with an envelope and a warning to never put him in that position again. I don't know how he managed it, but within the envelope was a new i.d. card, a letter of transfer, saying that I had been moved from my previous role and was to start work in the canteen area of your father's settlement. The contents of that enveloped offered me the chance of a new life.

The following morning, I was so nervous leaving the house with your father for the first time in two months and made my way to the canteen area to report for duty. I held my breath as my card was scanned by the guard, fearing being dragged away to be dealt with properly. However, nothing happened. The guard had to ask me to keep moving, such was my shock, and so I began working in the canteen and living with your father. Finally my life was back on track again, or so it seemed.

A few days later I began to feel deeply unwell. Severe aches and pains, sickness and flu like fever. I recognised the symptoms immediately, having seen many other girls with them over the last few years but initially tried to deny it to myself. When I quickly became too ill to work, guards came to the house to check on me. Unsure what to say, your father once again stepped in to save me by telling them I was pregnant with his child and was suffering from pregnancy related issues. They accepted this after a health worker confirmed that I was indeed pregnant and gave us both clearance to miss work whilst I was so unwell.

It was a hard time for us a couple, as true feelings for each other had started to develop, only for a pregnancy to intervene and one that would most likely take my life too. But credit to your father once again as he never complained or changed his mind once during the ordeal and against all the odds I somehow survived and gave birth to a beautiful, healthy baby boy. You my son.'

'How did you manage to survive when all the others didn't?' I ask.

'I don't know the reason for that for sure, but I think it was down to two things. Your father's love and support and the fact that it was no ordinary baby growing inside me. It was something rather special indeed, a fighter, even back then, equal to no one.

You may not have been your father's child biologically, but you certainly were in every other aspect and he treated you as such from the moment we knew I was pregnant. We both owe our lives to your father.'

I smile appreciatively towards my dad, who smiles warmly in return.

'He never once asked for anything in return,' continues Mom. 'And although we were a couple to the outer world, it was only after you were born did our relationship progress beyond friendship into a loving one. By the time we applied for a marriage certificate, it was for real, as was your life as you know it.'

Story finished, my mom looks at me nervously, unsure as to what my reaction will be, but she needn't have been apprehensive. What could you possibly feel but admiration and respect for your parents coming through all that? I pull my mom in close and give her the biggest hug ever, before signalling for my father to join in.

Chapter 36

A short while later, as myself, my parents and the superior squeezed into the Mustang, you could still hear the noise of the crowd echoing down from the colosseum above. Driving out of the arena, there were no guards to be seen, but plenty of ordinary citizens celebrating wildly.

The moment they see the Mustang exiting, they flock towards it in their droves, blocking the road out as they crowd around the vehicle, shouting my name and banging on the car. I have to crawl forward in order to avoid running over anyone. Despite the fact they were celebrating my victory, it was beginning to get a little unsettling, such was the frenzy and when we finally manage to pull free of them and speed away, I think everyone felt a bit relieved.

Just as we are starting to relax again, my dad pipes up, 'Is that smoke coming from the arena?'

Between glancing back and looking in my mirrors, I can see a thick black plume of smoke billowing into the clear sky, that certainly gave the impression it was indeed coming from somewhere inside the arena. What the hell was happening?

The training camp is eerily quiet on return and when we arrive at the apartments, it feels like we are in a kind of strange limbo. I desperately want to see Petra. Firstly, just because I want to see and be with her, but also to find out what happens now? What was Cero and the other Gods reactions to what had unfolded during the contest?

Unfortunately, I would have to wait until the early hours of the night before I see the apartment light up red from the window as I sit outside alone with my thoughts and the view of the stars. The others had gone inside to get some rest after a long day, particularly my parents, who looked understandably, mentally shattered.

The moment I notice the red light, I rush back inside my apartment to find Petra standing in the middle of the living room. We both smile with joy and relief before embracing each other warmly.

'That was quite the display, God like, some would say,' says Petra when we eventually break apart.

'I told you you'd still to see the best of me,' I reply smugly.

'Yes, you've certainly shown everyone now. Are you even aware of what that display of ability means?'

'If you're referring to the fact that Cranock was my biological father, then yes, I am now. I wasn't when I entered the arena earlier however. Were you?'

'No, I knew you were different when I witnessed you destroy my army. In particular, the moment you advanced beyond your own army and charged straight through your opposite number. He was a highly skilled and experienced gladiator. Not someone I'd expect to succumb to defeat so quickly and easily, but the speed in which you charged into him would have been similar to that of a vehicle crashing into someone.

You didn't move as fast as you did today but it was certainly quick enough for me to take note.'

'That's not why this started, is it?' I ask, suddenly feeling a little crestfallen.

Petra laughs, before placing a hand on my cheek. 'Do not worry my dear that has nothing to do with what happened between us, relax,' which I did.

'You peaked my interest but not for a second did I jump from that to thinking we may share the same DNA. It is not open subject between the Gods of Cranock's passion for the younger human females, nor is it a well-kept secret either. But we knew from our research done many years ago that the DNA of our two species was not compatible and therefore a mixed-race child would be impossible. This is probably why Cero did not question his activities further. It appears evolution has progressed much quicker than we would have expected.

I was intrigued by you, not suspicious.'

'Good to know,' I reply with a grin. 'What do Cero and the others make of it all? Will we be left alone in peace now?'

Petra's face said it all. 'Yeah didn't think so somehow.'

'It's not that he's said as much, but now that he's aware of who or what you are, it will have definitely changed his mind set. Cero is not one to rush anything. He is clever and methodical and will take some time to think over what his next move will be.'

'And the other two?'

'Not so much, but they obviously know where my loyalties lie now, so I doubt much would be decided in my presence. Most likely they will be in discussion over the matter now that I am here.'

'Are we just expected to sit around and wait until they make a decision?' I ask incredulously.

'I know it's frustrating but we need to know where we stand with them before deciding the best way forward.'

'After today, we should be telling them what's what, and if they don't like it, I'll take them down too!'

'Ever the fighter,' laughs Petra. 'It may well come down to that, but that is not a battle to take on recklessly. Now that Cero knows what you are capable of, he won't take you so lightly again. It just depends whether he sees you as a potential ally or enemy.'

'Should we be looking over our shoulders?'

'No, we should be safe for now. Cero doesn't operate like Cranock, he wouldn't send a team to attack your parents or you for that matter. If he decides to move against us, he will do it face to face.'

'Yeah, I'll take your word for it,' I reply sarcastically. 'So, what do we do meantime?'

'I have a few ideas,' Petra's says as she leans in and plants her luscious lips on mine.

'That's the best thing you've said since you arrived,' I whisper through kisses as we stumble our way towards the bedroom.

Chapter 37

Petra left late the following morning to seek out the other Gods and try to find out what the previous night's discussions had amounted to, leaving the rest of us to sit for the remainder of the day, stuck in limbo. The training camp as a whole was eerily quiet, with the odd person wandering in looking like they had been out all night. When one of the gladiators that lived a few apartments down from me arrived home mid-afternoon, I shouted over, asking what was going on.

He began laughing, 'You should know, you started it.'

It was early evening, when Petra returned. 'So?' I enquired as she walked out of the apartment to join us while we enjoyed the last rays of sunshine before sunset.

'He wants to meet with you?' she replied.

'When?'

'Now.'

I glance around at the others and shake my head. 'He knows I'm here right?' I ask turning to face Petra once more, who nods sharply.

'Well tell him if he wants to speak to me he knows where to find me.'

'Believe me, I understand your annoyance with him but if we want to find out where we stand I think we should go, otherwise you can squabble and play who goes to who and waste several more days sitting around wondering what if?'

I sigh and look towards the others again. The superior shrugs his shoulders and gives me a 'who knows,' look.

My parents look at each other before my dad turns towards Petra.

'Will it be safe enough?' he asks.

'It will. He has assured me he just wants to talk. I trust his word,' replies Petra.

'Well I don't, but I'll trust yours. Go to the meeting son, sooner we sort things out the better.'

'Fine, but just a minute,' I say to Petra, rushing by her into the apartment, before returning with the two swords she gave me, holstered in my back sheath that I'd adjusted earlier in the day.

'Okay, let's go then.'

'I don't think you'll be needing them tonight.'

'Perhaps not but they'll give me peace of mind, just in case.'

'Very well, ready?'

I nod, before Petra reaches out to touch me and we disappear in a flash of red light.

'Thank you for agreeing to speak with me.'

I hear the voice but my eyes are still shut momentarily as my head spins and I fight the urge to heave. Still not a fan of that mode of transport.

'And you have my word, there will be no need to use your weapons today.'

As the spinning and urge to be sick fades, my eyes open and focus on where the voice is emitting from. Cero stands at the far side of a hall I immediately recognise from where I recently confronted Cranock within the great pyramid.

'That remains to be seen,' I reply, as my gaze spots Ti'ar and Dalip lingering not too far behind Cero.

'We are all friends here, or at least we can be. But perhaps until a little trust has been gained, just you and I could speak alone?' he asks, sensing my unease.

I look towards Petra for her thoughts. She nods in agreement.

'Very well,' I reply.

Cero signals to Ti'ar and Dalip who cast me less than friendly looks but leave as instructed. Petra smiles at me reassuringly before following the pair. Only once the large double doors close behind them loudly, does Cero begin to pace slowly towards me.

'It has been a very, very, long time since I admitted I was wrong about something or apologised for anything, but today I offer you both of these things. Firstly, I couldn't have been more wrong in assessing your ability and the threat you posed, in particular to Cranock. And secondly, I must apologise for the way in which you have been treated recently and for the manner in which I may have spoken derogatorily about you in the lead up to the contest, which of course, was only said because we believed you to be a human at the time.'

Cero paused as if waiting for a response, however, I wasn't sure what to say at the moment. I certainly hadn't expected him to start with an apology and equally I wasn't sure if I was prepared to accept it, so I remained silent for the time being.

'That may still sound rather derogatory, as you still share human DNA but let me explain. My words and actions were actually part of a much grander plan that would help to prevent the deaths of many humans. I don't believe you either meant to, or were aware of what your actions might have set in motion.'

'If you're referring to an uprising, Petra did mention it, but I fail to see any connection between that and trash talking me,' I say, finally breaking my silence.

'And that's my point in essence, for you see it wasn't really about trash talking you in the first place, it was merely a simple mental strategy, designed to start chipping away at the belief, hope and confidence you had already built up within the humans.

Just by daring to challenge a God in the manner that you did, suddenly had the human race daring to dream of something they had not realistically thought about in a long time. I merely counter acted your actions to try and curb the optimism, so that when the contest arrived and you were brutally and easily slaughtered by Cranock, any dream or thread of optimism would be completely drained from the entire human race and life could settle back down into its normal routine.

That didn't happen of course, as we were all caught off-guard by your abilities and as a result of that, my plan completely backfired. The human race has been empowered in the belief that they will soon be free of their constraints altogether by their new hero. A gladiator so powerful he can even defeat the Gods. Of course, what they don't realise yet is that you are as much one of us as you are one of them.

You have to marvel at the evolutionary process. We have studied many planets and species, including Earth and the humans, for a very long time and for the most part, the chain of evolution moves along slowly and gradually. However, every now and again, it takes a sudden, giant leap forward in the blink of an eye, advancing a species or race well ahead of their projected trajectory. Even with all the data we have, it is still both unpredictable and unexplainable. It is God like.' Cero adds, with a wry smile.

'When we first arrived, we knew genetically speaking, a mixed species birth would be impossible, at least to begin with. Evolution always catches up eventually, but generally never as quickly as this. Even giant leaps forward only tend to start happening after a certain length of time, usually far greater than the time that has passed since we landed here on Earth.

And so, the outcome of which, is that you managed to slip by, unnoticed by all of us until it was too late. Or too late for Cranock at least, I should say. Do you have any feelings over the fact that you killed your biological father?'

'No,' I reply flatly.

Cero looks at me, then makes a face that implies he was expecting me to say more on the subject.

'Anyway, it appears evolution's latest giant leap has made something very special indeed. I have to admit to being more than a little intrigued to learn what you are fully capable of.'

'Perhaps you will one day,' I say, returning the wry smile.

Cero laughs in reply. 'Yes, I do hope so, albeit in a rather different manner to the way Cranock learned. It certainly seems that you have picked up the better traits each of our species have to offer as opposed to the bad ones. That said, no one is ever truly perfect.'

'I agree with you there.'

'Yes, I'm sure you do. Petra tells me you have remained semi isolated at the training camp since the contest. Are you even aware of what has been happening out there since your victory?' asks Cero, motioning towards the glass walled side of the dimly lit hall.

I wander across to the viewing area and cast my gaze across the far-reaching land. Too intent in watching Cero like a hawk, I hadn't even noticed the many, dark plumes of smoke billowing into the eerie, sunset red skyline.

'What's with all the fires?' I ask.

'Oh, it's not my doing. It's the humans lighting them in the settlements, on the building sites, on the roads and forests, even the colosseum was targeted in the aftermath of your contest.'

'Why?'

'Because they think they have been set free. Your victory was the catalyst, in their eyes, a human defeating a God. They expect you to kill us all now and return the Earth to the rule of humans. The fires are a demonstration of defiance. You have empowered the people and their behaviour will continue to escalate. They believe they are on the cusp of a new era and all the rules of the Gods need not apply anymore.'

'I'm sure you have the means to make them think otherwise.'

Cero laughs once more. 'Yes, of course I do, but I'm not going to. At least not for a while yet and I'll tell you why.'

'Please do.'

'From this point on, your life will inevitably come down to two choices or paths if you like. Whether you want to be or not, you have established yourself as the leader of an uprising. The humans expect you to go on and lead them to freedom and rid them of the Gods' rule forever, which is path one. Before choosing this path however, I want you to see the true nature of the human race when they are allowed to live unrestrained by strict rules.

Humans long to be free, when in fact they have not roamed free for thousands of years. They might have thought of themselves as being free before we arrived but they were not. They were bound by the rules of the rich and powerful, kings and queens of the olden days to the modern politicians and presidents. Human minds are fickle, they believe they have free speech only to be told what is allowed to be said and what is not. Work hard, then hand over vast sums of your earnings to the powers that be under the guise of services provided, whilst they laced their pockets with ridiculous sums of money and paid not a penny towards the very things everyone else must.

People believe we took over the Earth and destroyed it, when in actual fact we saved it. We saved the planet from being bled dry of its natural resources and minerals. We gave human kind a purpose other than the false lure of money. Humans think our laws are hard and tough, but they don't realise they need this. Our laws protect them from themselves as you will witness very shortly.

Rapists, murderers, child abusers, to name but a few of humankind's despicable crimes that they committed on a daily basis, yet now are virtually unheard of. The perpetrators of these crimes would not receive the proper justice, with weak laws and even weaker leaders unable or unwilling to take the measures necessary.

Our law is strict but fair. Commit a heinous act of such and you will pay the price with your life, no ifs or buts. The fear of the penalty and the penalty itself soon weeds out those unable to abide by these laws and now we live in a virtually crime free society. Are we praised for such actions? Of course not.'

'When you arrive on a planet and destroy most of its infrastructure and wipe out half the population, I guess folk find it hard to move on,' I say sarcastically.

'Yes, the human's small mindedness struggles to cope with making hard decisions and sacrifices and as such they cannot comprehend the true facts of what we actually did when we arrived. As I've already mentioned, Earth as a planet was dying. It had reached a critical stage and had we not intervened, the planet would have tipped over the point of no return and died, along with everyone and everything on it.

Such was the human greed for money and wealth, and disregard for the planet, they had even poisoned the very air we all need to breathe, again almost to the point of no return.

Our actions on the so-called landing day, may have been brutal and catastrophic, but that is the actions that were required to save the planet and the native species on it. Obviously, we had to send a message of dominance out there as well. No one arrives and takes over a planet with words and small actions, so that played its part too I concede, but there were also other reasons for the action we took.

We destroyed every major city in the world because the population required culling and major cities tend to contribute the most pollution to the atmosphere.

The world was vastly over populated and yet no one was strong enough to take the action needed. Instead the population was allowed to continue breeding at an unprecedented rate. Even when there was enough food to go around, was it shared? No, of course not. Not while the rich and greedy gorged themselves and poorer children literally lay dying of starvation. Who starves now? No one, that's who. We have an equal society that never starves. All you are required to do is contributing in your own way to help the greater society. Does that seem like a lot to ask for in return for never having to worry about starving or a place to live?

Humans are still allowed to have partners and families and enjoy love in their life. We limit children to one per family, to ensure the planet never becomes anywhere near the atrociously over populated state it was in previously.

The weak leaders of the world deserved to pay the price for the sheer negligence and greed they have shown in equal measures and that is why we made a very personal display of dealing with them. But from the ashes, we have a world where leaders are strong and live and die by their own actions and words, like you for example.

Tell me honestly, up until recent events, how would you describe your life? Would you say you felt hard done by? A slave to ungrateful, unrewarding Gods? A victim of crime and hunger? Or was your upbringing free from these elements, before finding your calling in life? Having it nurtured, pushed to find the limits of excellence. Becoming a champion. Was that enjoyable? To perform in front of thousands of cheering fans?'

My life was full of a bit more than just that when you broke it down, but I grudgingly had to admit he had a point. Until recent events with Cranock, if asked whether I'd led a good life or not, I would say yes, without a shadow of a doubt. My childhood had been fun and free of any hardships, until I came of age and started with the builders. That was the only time I could look back on my life and say I was deeply unhappy, and yet strangely if I was asked to change it, I'm not sure I would. Perhaps I needed the toughening up and hardships that my old crew cast upon me, to set me on the path I had eventually led.

Had I not tasted the bitterness would I have applied myself to the armed forces in the same manner which I had. Maybe, maybe not. And since the days of the building site, looking back, I enjoyed and revelled in every minute of the training and subsequent gladiator contests that followed.

'Well?' prompted Cero.

'Yes, I concede your point. I've enjoyed my life and wanted for nothing as a child.'

'You see, and for your exemplary service to your God, were you not rewarded well?'

'I was, at least until it was all taken away from me undeservedly.'

'Yes well, perhaps that highlights my point that no one is perfect. We try to be fair but that is not always the case. You were mistreated by Cranock, for which I have already acknowledged and apologised for.

Moving on, your actions in the arena bring me to another point. They won't admit it, but humans have a blood lustful nature. They feign horror and anger over our actions on landing day and yet were more than happy to either take part in or turn a blind eye to atrocities that were being conducted every single day around the world for thousands of years before we came. The ancient

Romans, recognised this too, controlling the mob as they termed it, by giving them what they wanted. Blood and gore. It worked well, only to be abolished under the guise of religion. We have taken advantage of both, by giving the world the Gods they so desired and keeping them happy with the blood and gore of the modern-day colosseums.

For those with the greatest blood lust, we harness it and give them focus and direction, eventually moulding them into great warriors such as yourself. It's something you would probably have never been aware of, but had you lived in the pre-God era, without the direction and outlet we provide, you would have most likely lost control of the rage and bloodlust that resides deep within you. That is why so many prisons existed before. Incarcerating millions of men and woman at a cost to themselves and to the greater society. Financially, mentally and physically.

There is not a single prison to be found on our New Earth, because we understand how to nurture the beast if you like and if that's not possible, we deal with the problem quickly and severely.'

'Alright, I get it,' I say holding my hands up. 'You've made your view clear on what you think of the human race. I'm guessing there's a point to telling me all this?'

'Indeed, there is,' replies Cero with a wry smile once more. 'Which brings us to path two. The path in which I very much hope you will decide to take.'

'And where will this path lead me to?'

'To greatness, in short.'

'Sounds wonderful,' I reply sarcastically. 'Try me with the long version.'

'Join us and become a God. Take your rightful spot and claim the throne of your late father. It is in your blood after all, at least in part and you have proven yourself to be more than worthy. You will take what was Cranock's, and rule over North America or perhaps unite with Petra and rule over the whole of the Americas as one. This very pyramid we stand within right now, will be yours in its entirety.'

'Sounds too good to be true. What's the catch?'

'The human uprising will obviously come to an end. Many of them will need to be made an example of and although you will rule over this land, you will do so abiding by the laws that I command. There will be no changing the current way of human life and if our laws are not adhered to, the same severe penalties will be applied by your hand. Until such times that I and the other Gods are satisfied your loyalty truly lies with us.'

'And if I'm unwilling to do as you ask?'

'Then you have chosen to take the first path.'

'What is with the paths? I fail to see why I need to be either an uprising leader or a God.'

'You don't now, but you will. It might be hard to understand, but it is inevitable that your life will come down to the two choices I have spoken of.'

I opened my mouth to object, but Cero raises his hand to silence me. 'Please, objecting will only be wasting your breath. A plan has been set in motion that will make this decision unavoidable, but I do not expect you to give me an answer just now. You will have one week from today. All I ask of you during this time is to observe what you see with your own eyes before coming to a decision. As I've said already, I will refrain from curtailing the human's activities and allow you to witness what transpires. Does that sound fair enough?'

I laugh. 'About as fair as you can get when someone makes you choose between one option and the other.'

'Yes quite,' replies Cero. 'Myself, Ti'ar and Dalip will be leaving now. Your living quarters within the pyramid are now yours once again. I'm sure you'll find them more pleasant than the limited accommodation at the training camp. The adjoining apartments are also vacant, should you wish for your parents and the guard that has been protecting them to join you. You will have access to all but the upper echelons of the building, of which will become available if you decide to join us. We will return in one week to find out the answer to that and see how the land has fared in our absence. Until then, I bid you farewell Jacob, son of Cranock.'

The last part makes me cringe, and all I can muster is a simple nod in reply, before Cero heads for the large double door and leaves me in the hall alone. Darkness has fallen as I gaze out the window across the land but the smoke plumes are still visible as dark shadows in the distance. I wasn't sure what to think after that meeting. It sure as hell wasn't the chat I was expecting to have.

An invitation to join the ranks of the Gods themselves, albeit with conditions attached, was still a surprise nonetheless. However, the overriding message was clear, pick one species or the other.

Chapter 38

Another hour passes by before Petra joins me in the hall again, but such were the magnitude of thoughts running through my mind, it barely feels like five minutes.

'Well, how did it go?' asks Petra in that sultry voice of hers, snapping me from my thoughts.

I turn to look at her and can't help but be blown away by her beauty, even in the dim light of the hall. 'Are you aware of what he proposed?'

'Yes I think so, he just shared the main points with me at least,' replies Petra.

'And?' she prompts, when I fall silent.

'I'm not sure what to make of it or whether we can even trust him. Can we?'

'If Cero has promised something, I would say his word is good for it. That said however, he can be coy with choosing what information he decides you need to know.'

'For example?'

'For example, I believe you have been given one week to decide your answer but do you know how that will be done?'

'I'm not sure what you mean?'

'A new contest has been announced.'

'A gladiator contest? For who? When did that get announced?'

'Yes, a new gladiator battle for the current champion, you! It was announced to the world whilst you were in here meeting with Cero. It will be held one week from today.'

I began laughing sarcastically. 'One week from today, really? I'm beginning to get the picture now. And who is my opponent to be?'

'Me,' replies Petra with a wry smile.

'What? You, really?'

'Yes, I'm afraid so.'

'I don't understand. Dalip, Ti'ar, even Cero himself, yeah sure, I would be happy to take either of them on, but you. Does he actually expect me to fight you?'

'No, probably not, but it isn't that surprising when you think about it. It's not really about you and I fighting each other as it is more a test of loyalty. He's testing my allegiance as much as yours. If I flat out refuse to enter the arena, he will know immediately I have been lost to his command and I can no longer be trusted. If I take to the sand then the onus moves onto you. If you choose to join us, then that is where you will very publicly decree your loyalty to the Gods, ending your hero worship status amongst the humans and with it any hopes they had of an uprising.'

'And by announcing the fight to the people, he more or less takes away the option for me to refuse the contest, because no matter what way I decide, both sides will expect me to be there to make a statement on their behalf,' I say.

'Exactly, now you're getting the full picture.'

'He's certainly factored in the options should I side one way or the other but what if we do neither? The only side I'm concerned about is yours. What if we meet in the arena but instead of fighting each other, we turn on the other Gods?'

'The only problem with that is the moment our intentions became obvious, we would probably be blasted out of existence from the sky, along with everyone else in the arena,' replied Petra pointing towards the huge ship I now knew hovered high in the sky above us.

'Unless we took that out the equation beforehand. You mentioned it required two Gods to do so?'

'It does, but it's not quite as simple as that, it's linked to the chips in our head so it wouldn't work with you, despite your new found DNA I'm afraid.'

'No, I didn't think it would, I was just wondering whether a certain dead God's head would suffice?'

Petra smiled. 'It might, but is that really the way we want to go? For starters, even with the threat from above nullified, taking on the remaining Gods will not be easy, particularly Cero. He was and I guess still is our leader for good reason. He would be a far more formidable opponent than Cranock, as would Dalip and Ti'ar.

His methods can be a little perplexing, but Cero's word is trustworthy. If you choose to accept it, I believe we would be left alone to rule over the Americas as we see fit. Does that sound like such a bad deal?'

'Not when you say it like that, but that wasn't quite the same way I heard it from Cero. There were conditions. We still have to answer to his command and he made it clear a heavy price would have to be paid by the humans for their revolt and it would be by my hand. What does that mean? Do I need to slaughter hundreds or even thousands of humans for daring to dream of a better life?'

'And if it did, would that not be a price worth paying to live the rest of your life, *our life*, as Gods and rulers?'

'Perhaps for you, but up until a few days ago, I was one of those humans. My parents are humans. I'm still part human. I don't know if that's a price I can live with.'

Petra places her warm hand on my face. 'I understand. I do not mean to push you into a decision, I'm merely laying out all the facts and options. Just know that whatever you decide, I will stand beside you my love.'

We kiss for a moment, before Petra adds. 'Before you make any decisions, I have some things to show you, but we have time for now, so why don't we relax and unwind a little tonight, start afresh tomorrow.'

'Yeah that sounds good to me. I don't think I could handle any more information right now. Also, I can't wait to get my old apartment back and watch a good movie or two,' I say with a large smile forming on my face.

Petra laughs and again I can't help but admire her beauty.

'Yes, I have to admit to missing those myself. Do you want to collect your parents and the guard and show them to their new accommodation first? I'm sure they'll appreciate the upgrade, then we can settle in for the night?' asks Petra, holding her hand out for me to take.

'Perfect,' I reply, as I accept her hand and we disappear in a ball of blinding red light.

Chapter 39

After filling in my parents and the superior on our meeting, my mother is understandably hesitant about returning to the great pyramid. Many years have passed since she was last there, but I guess those kinds of mental scars never heal. Only after assuring her the only God to be present will be Petra and a subtle reminder that I'd removed Cranock's head from his body, does she agree to return.

The superior is the complete opposite, and can't wait to check out his new deluxe apartment. After another stomach-churning journey through time and space, I tell Petra I'll just drive the Mustang and meet her back at the great pyramid.

She laughs before calling me something under her breath and disappearing. With barely any belongings between the remaining four of us, it isn't long before we're all squeezed into the Mustang, enroute back to the great pyramid.

Approaching the grand building, I notice my mother looks visibly apprehensive but remains quiet and there has been a noticeable increase in the amount of armed forces around the perimeter. Once inside, we head straight for the apartments, with the superior looking like an excited child ready to explore and myself keen to show my mother into her apartment, which will hopefully make her feel a little more at ease.

It appears to do the trick, and I leave my parents enthralled after a quick demonstration on how to play music and films. The superior clearly knew how they worked, as I can hear music being played extremely loudly when I pass his apartment in the hallway.

I'm relieved to finally reach my own apartment, keen to unwind after another long day. Entering, a smile forms on my face when I hear the unmistakable voices from the film Forest Gump. Petra's favourite. I stroll over to the couch and fall into her arms. I have much to think about, but that can wait till tomorrow.

Chapter 40

I won't lie. It is nice to have the luxury of my old apartment back. The view, the space, the extras. They feel good. After watching the remainder of Forrest Gump for the third time, we retire to a nice, spacious bed and have the best night's sleep I've had in a while.

After waking and showering, I collect the others and make our way to the nearest canteen area. Upon entering, silence falls over the few workers that are eating, unsure how to act, before they jump to their feet in a show of respect.

'It's alright, carry on, eat your breakfast,' I say, trying to return things to normal, but it was clear my presence was having an effect on many of them. We ate nonetheless then returned to the apartments to meet Petra, who had said it was beneath her to eat around the workers. I'd laughed when she had said that, but after our own awkward experience, I realise that perhaps she had a point, if it made it less awkward for all concerned.

If I chose to accept Cero's offer, we'd soon be dining by ourselves in the upper echelons of the pyramid anyway.

Petra said it was time for her to show me what Cero wanted me to see and so grudgingly, I took her hand and waited for my stomach to be whisked away from me.

When the red light vanished, I noticed two things. Firstly, the journey had proven to be a little less horrific this time around and secondly, I was now back in space, aboard the Gods' vessel.

'Cero wants you to properly understand the human race before you make any decision, and to do that he would like you to take a look through some of the huge amount of data we have recorded on the humans, over many, many years.'

'Exactly how much data are we talking?' I reply.

'Far more than could be crammed into a week, but I'll try my best to show you the more relevant content.'

'Alright, show away then.'

'Over this way, take a seat,' instructs Petra, guiding me towards another area of the craft, where a singular smooth looking seat, lay strangely in the middle of the room. I sit down and almost immediately the seat rolls backwards lifting my feet off the ground. At the same time, the smooth material it is made from begins to move and mould itself around my body shape.

'Whoooaaa,' I call out, startled.'

Petra laughs.

Now almost lying down, staring at the ceiling, I realise it was actually incredibly comfortable.

'Alright, what happens now?'

'Now it begins,' replies Petra.

Images suddenly began to pop up all around me until I become engulfed with a mixtures of noise and colour. I'm starting to feel dizzy when I hear Petra's voice above it all.

'Stay calm and try to focus. It will become clearer soon.'

I take her advice, closing my eyes for a moment to try and help focus my mind. It begins to work as the noise slowly settles down in to clear voices and when I re-open my eyes, the wave of colour is now a series of sharp images.

'Better?'

'Yes, much,' I reply.

'Watch and listen to as much as you can, but try not to let it overload you. Just tell me when you want a break, I'll be here.'

A virtual history of human life, pre-God era starts to unfold before me. I listen and learn intently for hours, becoming so engrossed in the various news reports, documentaries and other recorded information, I am unaware exactly how much time has actually passed by when everything suddenly disappears and I find Petra standing over me.

'Are you alright? That was quite a while for your first time.'

'Yes, I'm fine thanks, albeit I'm beginning to see Cero's point about being a bloodthirsty species.'

'Yes quite. I'm afraid there's still a long way to go, but take a break for now.'

After a short rest, the history lesson continued and before I knew it, day had turned to evening, or so Petra informed me. Hard to tell when you're in a spacecraft, but we returned to the great pyramid to eat and recover. It wasn't taxing physically, but certainly mentally I was beat and feel asleep almost as soon as I sat down on the couch to watch a film.

The following day, after breakfast, we returned to the space craft and resumed the lesson, spending the entire day there, and the following day. By the end of the third day, I called to Petra to turn it off.

'That's me I'm done with it. My head feels ready to explode.'

After three full days of supposed information gathering, I'd reached my limit. I could barely speak and went straight to bed on our return to Earth, sleeping through until the following afternoon.

I spent a long time in the shower, perhaps feeling the need to cleanse myself, before eating like a horse in the thankfully quiet canteen area. When I return to the apartment, I find Petra there.

'How are you feeling?' she asks.

'Well, let me see. Sad, angry, disappointed, shattered, suspicious.'

'I can imagine, it's a lot to absorb in such a short space of time. Has it affected your view on the human race as a species?'

'How could it not?' I reply, taking a seat on the couch beside Petra. 'As much as I don't trust Cero, he has a point on the human lust for war and violence. All they have done for their entire existence is fight with each other. War after war after war, it's never ending. From the ancient Vikings, to the Spartan warriors. The Athenians, Mongolians, the Crusades, Imperial China and ancient Egypt.

The Scots and the English, the English and the French. The English and everyone. Africa, where to begin there? Daily genocides, millions starving, dying from curable diseases and nobody cares.

Native Indians, the American civil wars, Vietnam, Iran, Iraq, Afghanistan. Russia, the Cold war. Yugoslavia. Germany, the world wars. South America, from ancient tribes to terror reigned down upon the region by the drug cartels.

The Middle East!

As a warrior and a gladiator I can appreciate the art of battle and the honour and pride in the glory, but most of these wars, brutal deaths and genocides, were committed under guises, such as religion, good versus evil, false information, they did this, they did that, your country needs you. When in actual fact, most of the time they were merely about filling the pockets of the rich and greedy. Making the powerful, more powerful. Many spineless leaders, sending millions to their death from the comfort of their own lavish house or office. Asking others to do what they would not themselves. And that's me just scratching the surface.

Then there's the smaller in scale crimes but equally barbaric. Literally millions of them committed on a daily basis. Murder, rape, child abuse, kidnap, assault, theft and fraud to name but a few, all done on a scale you wouldn't dream could be possible. Alcohol and drugs ravage through the population like a disease. Many have the cheek to call it that, such is the human weakness to accept responsibility for their actions. As a species, we must rank among the worst in the whole universe.'

'Believe it or not, there are worse out there, but not many. Yes, the humans are definitely not without fault. However, there is some good and truly kind at heart people out there, sadly they are just heavily outweighed by the not so good. I only showed you what Cero has allowed me to show you, which of course is the worst of humanity but there are many positives to the race too. Perhaps, one day I will be able to show that side, but for now you will just need to take my word for it.'

'Not easy to do after witnessing all that.'

'I'm not trying to excuse anything I'm just saying perhaps you shouldn't judge them too harshly until you have witnessed the full picture.'

I get what Petra is saying, but it's hard to shake off the three days of negative information I have just digested. I rise from the couch and wander across the windowed wall to gaze over the land. Even more plumes of black smoke drift into the sky from different settlements along the horizon.

'What's been happening out there?' I ask.

'The humans think they are free again and as Cero predicted, immediately falling into their old ways. The settlements are awash with unrest. Homes are being ransacked and torched. Beatings are taking place as grudges become settled with no fear of punishment. Guards were being attacked before they were ordered to withdraw from the settlements. Woman and children, are being forced into hiding, with no protection from the twisted element among their society that you just mentioned.'

I continue to stare in silence for a moment at the dark plumes of smoke in the distance, before finally saying, 'I'm going out tonight. I want to have a look at what's going on first hand.'

I then leave Petra to catch up on some much-needed physical training after spending the last three days glued to a chair.

It shows, as I'm sluggish to begin with but soon shake it off and go on to spend the remainder of the day training. By early evening I'm feeling refreshed and check in on my parents and the superior before leaving the great pyramid. On hearing my plans, the superior insisted on coming with me and soon we are leaving the building in one of the armed forces jeeps, deciding against using one of the flashier vehicles now at my disposal.

Upon nearing one of the closest settlements to the great pyramid we encounter a heavy armed forces presence, who flag down our vehicle on approach.

'Sorry sir, didn't realise it was you,' said the surprised looking guard at my window.

'What's going on soldier?' I enquire.

'Nothing really sir, our instructions are just to keep our distance for now, ensure the trouble doesn't spread out of the settlements and head towards the great pyramid. But as long as it stays in there, we've just to leave them be.'

'We'll go on foot from here then,' I say to the superior exiting the vehicle.

'You're going into the settlement sir?' asks the guard.

'We are indeed.'

'You sure that's wise sir?'

I give the guard a curt look, which he responds to.

'Sorry sir, didn't mean to question your actions. It's just that things are getting a little out of hand in there. Would you like a team to escort you?'

'No soldier, we'll be fine.' Is the last thing I say before the superior and I begin marching beyond the line of armed forces vehicles as we head towards the settlement.

Chapter 41

Approaching the settlement, I raise my hood to hopefully avoid recognition and the need to deal with any unwanted attention it may bring.

'Don't think I'll need to worry about that,' laughed the superior, reading my thoughts.

Passing the first houses, everything was quiet, vacant looking, but as we progress deeper into the settlement, the noise levels rise. Singing, shouting and cursing can all be heard. Movement in the shadows to our left makes us both spin around, just as a family emerge and nearly crash into us. The man immediately pushes his child and wife behind him.

'Apologies men, we didn't mean to startle you. We'll be on our way,' he says, eyeing us suspiciously.

'What's going in there?' I ask.

The family just look at us like we're crazy, until I remove my hood and show my face. 'Do you know who I am?'

'Of course sir,' replies the man, bending his knee.

'Stand, there's no need for that and no need to fear us. Please, tell me what's been happening in the settlements.'

'It's chaos sir. It all started off with celebrations after your victory over Cranock. Everyone was out in the streets, cheering and singing, thinking or hoping that it signalled the beginning of a new era. When the Gods or the armed forces didn't intervene, things just grew and grew until they were out of control. It went from small fires being lit to keep us warm at night, to whole houses being destroyed and set alight. People are drinking openly on the streets. Intoxicated and angry, is not a good combination. Folk are fighting, even killing each other over nothing. Just years of frustration boiling over. It's not just here, bad elements from other settlements have been roaming around intent on causing trouble in whichever settlement they reach next, taking advantage of the fact that the armed forces are just sitting back and allowing it to happen.

We had to flee our own home, as the lunatics set it alight and laughed as we ran from the burning building. It's madness.'

'Where are you going now?' I ask.

'My parents' house, they still live on the outskirts of the settlement, away from the chaos in the centre of it.'

'Thank you, get your family to safety then.'

'I will sir, take care.'

As the man and his family set off, the superior looks at me with a grin and says, 'This should be interesting.'

It's not long before we begin to encounter homes ravaged with fire, some are still burning, others just blackened shells. A rather intoxicated looking man stumbles across our path, before puking his guts up nearby. Another two follow, paying little attention to us as they roar with laughter, mocking the man.

Further down the road, a fight has broken out between two men, which quickly grows as others run to join in. A living room window suddenly shatters, drawing our attention away from the rabble of the fight. A moment later, three men exit the house, one of them turning back to repeatedly kick the door. I pause to look at the trio, wondering what the attraction is to suddenly start destroying another person's home, when the man closest to me shouts something. I'm too lost in my thoughts to hear what he said, but as I turn towards him, I can tell by the snarling look on his face it wasn't friendly.

He approaches aggressively, opening his mouth to shout something else but in the blink of an eye my fist smashes into his face and knock's him out cold.

As his body crumples onto the ground, the other two men suddenly pause for thought. They're whole demeanour changes from aggressive to nervous in an instant, before they turn and run off, leaving their unconscious friend behind.

We continue on to the centre of the settlement, finding the streets awash with this type of behaviour. Feuding, fighting, ransacking and intoxication, all to the background of houses being burned to the ground. What was wrong with people?

The screams of a young female catch our attention and we set course to investigate. Rounding the corner of a new street we encounter two men attacking a young woman. As we approach, the larger of the two men, punches the female in the face causing her to fall to the ground, where he climbs on top of her and begins to rip her clothing free. The other male stands over them, laughing and egging his accomplice on.

The superior moves towards the group but I catch his arm. 'I've got this,' I say before rushing forward. The man on top of the girl doesn't even know I'm there until I grab him by the hair, yank his head back and slice his neck wide open with my dagger. I throw him off the girl then turn to his friend who is gawking at me open mouthed in shock.

I quickly shut that stupid mouth of his for him by thrusting my dagger under his chin and deep up into his face. He slumps down on the ground, beside the other man who is trying in vain to stem the flow of blood from his neck.

Helping the girl back to her feet, I ask, 'Are you alright?'

'I think so,' she replies, rubbing her jaw and wiping her tears.

'Do you have a home to go to?'

She nods.

'Show us the way then and we'll make sure you get there safely.'

The girl nods once again before replying 'Thank you.'

We escort her through the chaotic streets, avoiding any further confrontation, which is hard because I want to stop and teach every single person a lesson that I see acting in a manner that supports Cero's view of the human race, and we see a lot of them. However, in the interests of keeping the girl safe from harm, we decide not to engage with anyone, unless of course they were stupid enough to venture too close. For the few that did, they soon regretted it.

Before long we reach the girl's house and send her inside with instructions to lock the door and not to come out again tonight.

'The streets will be cleared of by sunrise, you have my word,' was my parting comment to the girl.

'Will they?' enquired the superior.

'They better be or heads will roll,' I reply. 'Come on, I've seen enough, let's get out of here.'

Upon leaving the settlement and approaching the armed forces line, the head guard comes to meet us. 'Soldier, that's a shit show in there. It gets sorted out tonight!

Round up the forces and get in there and make sure the other settlements are targeted too. I want everyone back in line by sunrise, understand?'

'Yes sir,' replied the guard but remained still. 'It's just, well…..'

'If there's a problem, spit it out.'

'Sorry sir, it's just that, well, our orders to stand by, came from Cero himself.'

I inhale a slow, deep breath before moving closer to the head guard.

'Soldier, I don't care who your orders came from. I'm in charge round these parts now, not Cero, and that kind of behaviour won't be tolerated under my watch. Do you understand that?'

'Yes sir.'

'Now, either you do as commanded or I'll relieve you of your position right now and get your next in command to do your job for you. What's it's to be?'

'Sorry sir, I didn't mean to question your command. I'll see to it right now and you have my word the settlements will be under control by morning.'

'Thank you soldier.'

'Yes sir.'

The head guard, then spun around and ran back to his troops, signalling and shouting orders as he went. Engines soon began to rumble and headlights lit up the darkness as all the armed forces vehicles readied themselves to enter the settlement. We watched them for a while as they took off into the rows and rows of housing to begin sorting out the dis-order. Once out of sight, the superior and I climbed into our jeep and set course for the great pyramid.

I found myself feeling angry on the journey back. Our expedition had proved to be everything I'd hoped it wouldn't. I knew there was good in the human race, my parents and the superior were evidence of that, but amidst what we'd witnessed first-hand tonight and all the information I'd absorbed over the last few days, it was becoming harder to argue with Cero's view, no matter how much I wanted to.

Chapter 42

The following morning, word was reported back to me that order had been restored to the settlements. Many had lost their lives during the process. However, from the behaviour I had witnessed first-hand, most that died probably deserved it anyway.

The next few days were spent within the confines of the pyramid, either training or watching a film as I tried to take my mind off things for a while. Finally, as darkness fell on the eve of the big day, I became restless, unable to keep my thoughts from tomorrow's event and still unsure on what to do. I wandered the halls of the great pyramid, becoming lost more than once, but ultimately finding myself back at the apartment no further forward. Petra had arrived during my walkabouts and began talking to me as I entered the apartment but I wasn't really listening to what she was saying.

I wandered across to the windowed wall and stood in silence, gazing out over the land. So lost in my thoughts, that I wasn't even aware of Petra's presence approaching until she stood right behind me. She slid her hands around my body until they became entwined in my own, then leaned in close and began to whisper into my ear.

Chapter 43

The noise was incredible. I closed my eyes and inhaled slowly, taking it all in one last time. The distinct smell of blood and sand, the sound of the crowd cheering your name. I almost yearned for my early days so I could do it all again and enjoy the glory of the arena. There truly was nothing quite like it. I wondered, after today, if the crowd would ever cheer my name again like they did right now.

The entrance door suddenly shot open, ending my moment, as heat and light streamed into the dark tunnel.

One last deep breath, then I stepped out onto the sand to a thundering roar from the packed colosseum audience. Petra was already occupying the centre of the sand, looking spectacular as usual, even from a distance. My gaze drifted from her to the baying crowd that surrounded us. Despite the armed forces bringing the recent unrest back under control, the crowd appeared undeterred, their fear of the Gods had still, rather unwisely, not returned.

I pause to look around at them closer, studying the individuals, you could see the venom in their faces and hear it in their voices, as they screamed for me to do all sorts of nasty things to Petra and the other Gods.

Never before had I seen or heard this kind of thing at any previous contest, but of course, that's simply because they wouldn't have gotten away with it. Any one of these venomous comments that were being shouted would have led to the punishment of death, no questions asked. It's amazing how things can change so quickly at times.

One man in particular catches my attention, a large, bald man, whose face has turned scarlet red, such were his actions and furious shouting.

'Slit her fucking throat,' he yells sliding his hand across his own in gesture. Even from afar, he was working himself into such a frenzy, I could see the spittle foaming out his mouth as he screams towards me.

'Rape the fucking bitch!'

Rape her? What the fuck was wrong with these people?

I turn away, shaking my head in dismay, as I continue on towards Petra.

Stopping a few yards from her, she smiles and says, 'I think the crowd are behind me today.'

'Yes, I noticed. You've a particularly charming fan back there,' I reply sarcastically, making her laugh.

A loud noise erupted throughout the arena, signalling for the crowd to be silent, which they complied with.

'Citizens of the New Earth,' began Cero's loud voice.

Petra and I continue to stare at each other for a moment before turning to face him as he addressed the arena and the millions watching on screens across the globe.

'Today's contest has been arranged as a consequence of the recent unexpected events. Jacob's victory over Cranock has led to some very misguided notion that the rule of the Gods is no more. Over the course of the last week, your abhorrent behaviour just goes to show that you have all sadly not shaken the sins of your past. Be under no illusion however, this was only allowed to happen because I permitted it. Even today, just moments ago, you have the audacity to dis-respect myself and the other Gods in such a blatant, personal and disgusting manner.

Now, you may be asking yourself, why have I allowed this behaviour to carry on relentlessly and unpunished, to the point you feel you are in such a position of power that you can disrespect the Gods to their faces?

Well believe me, you are going to find out very soon, but before we come to that, the saviour of the human race has a decision to make and I'd very much like to know the outcome of which. So, without further delay, let us begin with the contest. Jacob, our hero of the hour versus Petra, Goddess of South America.

Let the show commence!'

The crowd which had been muted, confused and a little worried during Cero's opening speech, suddenly erupted into life again. The roar was deafening as Petra and I turned to face each other once more. The crowd cheering my name and insulting the Gods in equal measure, despite Cero's warning just moments ago. Confidence must be really high amongst the humans of me truly ending the reign of the Gods.

'Well lover, what's it to be?' Petra asks with a sly grin on her face.

I reached over my shoulders and pulled my swords free from their sheath, signalling another huge roar of delight from the crowd.

Petra did likewise, as two glinting blue daggers suddenly appeared by her side.

I advance towards her, raising my swords, before spinning them around my grip in a fanciful show of swordsmanship. Nearing Petra, I bring them arcing down either side of her, striking them forcibly into the sand before stepping back, leaving the swords in place, handles pointing towards the sky. The crowd fall into a stunned silence when I go down on one knee in front of Petra.

Her daggers disappear, before I reach out and grasp her right hand.

'A little close there,' she whispers to me with a frown on her face that makes me smile.

'Sorry,' I reply, trying not to laugh as I kiss the back of her hand and bow my head in a show of loyalty.

Someone from the audience screams out,' Boooooooooooooooo.........!' Which acts as a signal for the rest of the crowd to shake off their shock and join in. The booing now rings out around the whole arena, along with all sorts of other kinds of abuse.

'SILENCE!' bellows Cero's voice eventually, ending the chorus of disappointment and anger.

'There you have it, plain for all to see. The so-called saviour of the human race has shown his loyalty, and rightly so, belongs with the Gods.

Part of the reason for this, is that he is not even one of you to begin with, for Jacob, hero of the humans, is actually son to the late God Cranock.

That's right earthlings, God's blood runs through Jacob's veins and as such, he will rightly follow in his true father's footsteps and join us in ruling over this New Earth that we have created.

Now, let me go back a moment to explain why I allowed this recent outburst of unrest and dis-respect to happen. As Jacob is obviously a child of the New Earth era, he has never witnessed humanity at its worst, when it is allowed to fester, with no rules or laws to obey and to run wild with no fear of punishment. After Cranock's death at the hands of Jacob, a feat which you all now know is still not possible by a mere human, it gave us an opportunity for Jacob to see you all at your worst. To see the real human race, with no guidance or Gods to obey. The slightest hope of being freed from our rule was enough to set you back years, and in the process demonstrate to Jacob, what is required under his command.

Because the unrest was allowed to spiral out of hand somewhat by myself, I will allow a slight level of leniency. However, I cannot and will not allow behaviour of this kind to go unpunished altogether, and be warned, the disrespect shown towards the Gods today in this arena will never happen again.

For those of you that escape any form of punishment from the recent misbehaviour, consider yourself extremely fortunate. Albeit, just because you leave the colosseum alive today, does not mean your actions won't catch up with you in the weeks to come.

For the time-being, take this little show as a very serious warning to any future conduct. Guards, bring them out!'

The entrance door that Petra would have stepped onto the sand from, suddenly shot open and out walked two guards, leading a line of five humans, whose hands were bound together behind their backs. Four more guards followed the prisoners, applying a rather less than gentle nudge to any of them that tried to slow the pace.

Noises of murmur began to emanate from the crowd, hesitant to boo or worse again after Cero's warning, but the looks on their faces said it all.

'These prisoners were found to be guilty of some of the more serious crimes committed over the last week and as such will be dealt with accordingly by their new God and ruler, Jacob.'

The minute Cero finished his sentence, I could feel the eyes of every human in the arena, staring down upon me, full of hatred and anger. In a heartbeat, I had gone from hero to villainous traitor.

Petra had warned me that if I chose this path, pledging my loyalty to the Gods would not be enough. Cero would plan some kind of display in front of both the humans and the Gods, to leave both sides in no uncertainty regarding my allegiance.

So be it. After what I had witnessed the other night, the men being punished were probably deserving of it anyway.

And I figured, if I was going to go the whole way, then what difference would another one make. I called over to a nearby guard and gave him some instructions. By now the five prisoners, were on their knees, in a line beside us, near the centre of the sand. I looked along the faces and recognised one of them from the unrest in the settlements. He was definitely guilty of something for sure. The silence that had fallen over the arena, was now broken by the shouting of one man, as he was dragged kicking and screaming from the crowd by the guards towards the rest of us.

'I didn't mean it. I'm sorry, I'm so sorry, please forgive me!' squealed the large red-faced man that had been shouting the vile things aimed at Petra.

I stepped towards him and sank a hefty punch into his body, which silenced him immediately and ceased the pulling and pushing he was doing with guards. As they now let go of their grip upon him, he fell to knees.

'Rape the bitch??' I say before crashing a hefty punch off his face, bursting his nose wide open on impact and sending him falling backwards onto the sand.

'Easy now there Jacob,' rang out Cero's loud voice. 'So keen to get on with things, but please allow me a moment to say a few words before we commence with the show.

Citizens of the New Earth, these men before you will now be dealt with by your God, Jacob, in any way he deems fit.'

I laugh inside at Cero's words. *As I deem fit.* The message was clear. I could turn around and free them if I wanted to, but both he and I knew that could not happen if I did not want to appear weak. To the humans however, it was my last chance. Spare their lives and allow them to cling to some kind of hope that I was still one of them really.

With every single set of eyes inside the arena, once again casting their gaze upon me, I lean over and pick the large man up by the scruff of his neck, hauling him up into the kneeling position. The face that had been consumed with anger and hatred only moments ago, was now full of shock and fear.

Whimpering and begging as I draw my dagger and hold it up to his face. He tries to pull away from me, but my grip is too tight and I hold him in place with ease. An inhumane noise fills the air as I press the tip of my dagger into one of his eyes and then slowly push it all the way in until the blade has completely disappeared. The noises he was making cease altogether before I let go of the grip I have upon his neck and allow his limp body to fall to the ground.

Before another word is said, I stride quickly towards the prisoners, drawing my swords in the process.

Reaching the first one, I slice his head clean off with my right sword, before crossing the left one over and sending the tip of it right into the side of the next prisoner's head. The third receives a sword through his heart, the fourth has half his neck removed, before the final prisoner has my sword driven down through his body from the base of his neck.

Six men dead in a matter of seconds and I now stand looking around at the stunned and silent arena. The Destroyer, gladiator champion, hero of the humans, was gone forever.

Chapter 44

Cero's solitary clap finally broke the silence hanging over the colosseum. 'A fine display Jacob, worthy of applause.'

When the arena remains silent, Cero's face erupts in a rare show of anger.

'APPLAUD.........' he shouts ferociously, provoking an immediate response.

The entire arena now claps for me, but it is an empty and hollow applause.

'Now,' begins Cero, putting the crowd out of their misery by ending the applause. 'Why don't you come up here and join us? Take your rightful place amongst the Gods.'

I sheath my swords and look across at Petra, who is already walking towards me with that sultry look of hers upon her face. She passes by the line of fresh corpses without the blink of an eye, before smiling and holding her hand out for me to take.

The moment I do, we disappear in a flash of red light, only to re-appear next to Cero, in the Gods' luxury viewing area.

'Welcome Jacob. You made a wise choice that I'm sure you won't regret.'

I smile and nod in reply to Cero.

'Your new God and ruler, Jacob,' Cero then announces to the arena, who start with the hollow applause once more.

'Take a bow Jacob, you earned it.'

It feels awkward, but I play the game and do as Cero instructs, bowing and waving to the crowd, despite the fact I knew none of it was real.

I'm relieved to finally sit down in my seat, which was in a row slightly behind Cero's, with seats for Petra, Dalip and Ti'ar. Sitting down, I glance across at the other Gods, receiving cold and unwelcoming looks in return from Dalip and Ti'ar.

Petra grabs my attention away from the others, entwining her hand in mine, happy to now show our affection for each other in public.

Cero then gives the order to commence with the other contests, a series of fights to celebrate the occasion, he says he'd arranged in the hope that my decision went the way it did.

It felt strange watching someone else take part in a gladiator battle, having been so used to being the one on the sand and if I'm being honest I had to hold myself back several times from wanting to run down there and join in. Old habits die hard.

When the last contest had finished, Cero spoke a few words to the crowd, finishing with another stark warning about future behaviour. All the Gods, including myself, courtesy of Petra then disappeared in the usual manner, re-appearing in a room I was becoming all too familiar with. The grand hall with the spectacular viewing area within the great pyramid.

'Congratulations Jacob. It's not often that an everyday street rat rises all the way up to becoming a God. A fine feat indeed,' Cero says in a slightly patronising tone.

I remain quiet, but notice the smirks on Dalip and Ti'ar's faces.

'Now do tell, what do you plan to do with all the humans and land that you now rule over?'

More smirks, louder this time from Dalip and Ti'ar. I glance over at Petra but she has her back turned, walking slowly away from me.

'Please, don't be rude,' Cero says to Ti'ar and Dalip, without conviction. 'Allow the son of Cranock to speak his mind.'

This only makes the pair smile further. I instinctively know something is off.

'If I may speak my mind, I must ask, what the fuck is going on here?'

This prompts a ripple of laughter, Cero included.

'Petra, what is this?' I shout towards her, noting she has continued walking across the hall in a looping meander, now passing behind Ti'ar and Dalip. As she does so, she glances across at me with a sly grin upon her face and asks, 'Do you really think you are worthy of becoming a true God my love?'

My hearts sinks and a horrible feeling passes through my body. Before I can reply, Cero speaks once more.

'The truth is Jacob, you did very well to pass through life without your true identity catching up with you. But the minute Petra first saw you in action when she and Cranock's armies met, she knew you were different. You were too fast and strong, to be human, at least fully human anyway, and quickly reported it to myself and the other Gods.

I have to be honest and say we were intrigued. I especially, wanted to find out a little more about you, which is the reason you weren't just taken out of the equation immediately. Cranock's indiscretions were not a secret, but we knew our DNA was not compatible either and it was still by all accounts too short a period of time for evolution to have taken place. However, as we spoke about previously, sometimes you get that jump which can surprise us all and so, I instructed Petra to get close to you and find out exactly who and what you were. A task that I'm sure you'll agree, was carried out immensely well.

You could even say, you were something of a science project for us and it's been a very long time since we've had one as interesting as this. The temptation to destroy you immediately was overwhelmed by curiosity. Did you know, the first time you kissed, you gave us access to your full genetic make-up, courtesy of that little chip in our head that you know about.

The minute your tongues connected and saliva was passed from mouth to mouth, Petra's magical little mind began processing your DNA.

I concede, it's a little gross sounding, but very informative nonetheless.'

I glance towards Petra once again, who continues to pace slowly around the hall, returning my gaze with a very smug and gloating look upon her face. I grit my teeth and look away.

'I must add that Cranock himself, was unaware of our little charade. The God like status we have been living here on Earth had gone to his head somewhat and began to give him questionable ideas of grandeur. Trouble was brewing in that fickle little mind of his as he sought to replace me as the God of Gods if you like,' says Cero, unable to hide the pleasure in his words, from his face.

I thought Cranock's ego was bad, but it was now becoming apparent it was a common trait amongst all of them. Living as Gods had fooled them into truly believing they were indeed Gods.

'You can see why we decided to keep our actions hidden from him for the time-being. Our next objective was to find out your true potential. Analyse your abilities and decide on whether you represented a threat to our existence as the dominant species on this planet.

Your own mounting squabbles with Cranock, presented the perfect opportunity right on our lap. When you burst into the arena and challenged Cranock to a contest, I couldn't have planned it better myself. It was all I could do to stop myself from laughing out loud, there and then at the complete irony of the situation and delight at the prospect of seeing you pitting your wits in the arena against Cranock.

For all Cranock's faults, his combat skills were exemplary. Petra may have played down his abilities to you, but that was just part of our plan. In truth, and as much as it pains me to say it, he was probably the most skilled warrior out of all of us. Of course, he should be really, for that was his expertise and the role he was chosen for, when we set off on our mission from our home planet many, many years ago.

And so, your challenge presented us with not only a mouth-watering contest to behold and a true test of your abilities, but also provided us with a win-win situation. No matter who won, it rid us of a potential problem.

It proved to be a spectacular occasion and if I'm being honest, not the outcome I had anticipated. I knew you had ability of course, but it turns out I grossly underestimated just how much you really had. You truly rose to the occasion and hit a level I didn't think you would be capable of. You rid us of one problem and revealed the true threat you presented to the rule we preside over this planet.'

'If we were both such a threat and problem to you, why not just take us both out quickly and easily from above, as you were supposedly ready to do with Petra and I?'
A chorus of laughter begins to echo around the hall.
'Oh, Jacob my love, that thing up is there is nothing more than a floating museum,' muses Petra.
'What?'
'It's still a little more than that, but in essence, she's right,' replies Cero. 'Our vessel, hasn't had the weaponry capabilities to destroy anything since we used everything it had on landing day. Petra's explanation of how we ended up on Earth is true. Our ship's power source was reaching its end, and unlike antiquated human weaponry, our ship's energy source, powered everything, weapons included. Can you even imagine the kind of power required to wipe out half the population and most of the infrastructure of a planet the size of Earth? I imagine not, but let me tell you, it's a lot. But it was also required in order to make the momentous changes the planet needed to survive. That we needed to survive.
To use up the last of our power resources in such a manner was undoubtedly a risk, but a highly calculated one that proved to be the correct course of action. The ship obviously still has residual energy left, not enough to weaponize or travel, but more than enough to enable

us to teleport and use other minor functions for many years to come.'

This time I laugh, which draws a peculiar look from Cero.

'It's all a con eh. You've been conning the people of Earth since the first day you all arrived. You most definitely aren't Gods. You aren't even superior beings. You think you are, but you're just the same as the scum I killed back in the arena. Yeah, that's it, five pieces of lying scum that have already ruled for far too long.'

Immediately several small flashes, accompanied with a humming noise signalled Ti'ar and Dalip had drawn their weapons, but I kept my eyes firmly on Cero, whose face bristled with anger. I take a little pleasure in knowing my comments have struck a chord of annoyance there.

'Easy now, don't let him get to you,' purrs Petra, upon reaching Cero and placing a gentle hand on his back, smoothly rubbing it from shoulder to shoulder.

Cero instantly regains his composure. 'Quite,' he replies, smiling ruefully.

'Tell me this, why bother going to all the trouble of announcing me as a new God and ruler, when it's now apparent that all you planned to do was kill me in the end anyway?' I ask whilst noticing Ti'ar has begun moving slowly around my right side in an effort to flank me.

'Yes, I can see why that might puzzle you. And I'm willing to share that information with you, I think you've earned that much at least,' replies Cero, in his full egotistical manner. 'As you know, our major weapon capability has ceased. We rely on fear of what may happen should the people revolt against our will, which if you'd witnessed the landing day devastation, works just fine. Along with strict laws and punishment should they be broken. Despite your misguided opinion, we are in fact, vastly superior beings to the average human and therefore could and will still rule over them should our lack of weapons secret ever surface. But it would be time consuming and laborious.

Your rise in prominence, gave hope to the humans. An uprising was born, especially after you defeated Cranock. Once started, it is not an easy thing to fix. We have witnessed many, and more often than not, they only continue to fester and grow. If we just killed you outright then, we would have created a martyr. The very thing that tends to push an uprising beyond the point of ever fixing. So, what's the best way of dealing with both issues? Use each problem to fix the other problem of course.

By making you one of us, and doing so in the manner that we did, any hero status you ever had amongst the humans has now well and truly died. Along with it, any hope of an uprising. To watch their hero butcher their own, was priceless. You even pulled an extra human out of the crowd and butchered him for insulting the most cold-hearted and ruthless person there.'

All the Gods roar with laughter, Petra included.

'I mean that in the nicest possible way of course my dear,' adds Cero.

'Of course,' she whispers affectionately over his shoulder, whilst staring directly at me. I try not to show a reaction on my face but can't help curling my fists into balls and squeezing as hard as I can in anger.

'Normal order has been restored and in the blink of an eye you have gone from hero, to being despised by all.

And now, we are free to kill you and no one will care one little bit,' says Cero as his famous curved bladed weapon suddenly appears in his grip and a look of malice falls over his face.

'Four against one?' I laugh. 'And you all have the cheek to preach on about honour and respect. Very well, if that's the way it's to be,' I add, glancing around to check Ti'ar's position before slowly pulling my swords free from the shoulder holster.

'To be fair, you were right about one thing,' I say.

'Go ahead then, indulge me with your last words,' replies Cero rolling his eyes at the inconvenience.

'Petra is without doubt, the most ruthless person in the room.'

A millisecond of doubt suddenly crosses Cero's face but it is too late. Petra's dagger like weapons light up behind him, slicing back and forward in a criss-cross motion as the long razor-sharp blades cut clean through Cero's neck, removing his head from his body.

The shock of what just happened was enough to distract Ti'ar's attention, long enough for me to take full advantage. Spinning around to face her, my left arm already in motion as it arcs around and throws one of my swords at the African Goddess. Her eyes hadn't even moved from the sight of Cero's shocking demise and the first she becomes aware of my attack is when my sword impales itself deep into her chest and sends her sprawling backwards onto the ground.

Her head has barely lifted off the ground when I'm upon her and duly waste no time in removing it from the rest of her body. I pull my sword free from her body and turn to face the last remaining threat.

Dalip was already busy defending himself from Petra, who had attacked immediately after dispatching of Cero. Dalip hadn't been caught off-guard as much as Ti'ar, and had managed to block Petra's attack and create a little space between them. He now raised his left arm and readied himself to send one of his deadly whips surging towards her.

Just as his arm was about to swing forward, my sword sliced clean through it near the shoulder joint, causing his whip to fall harmlessly to the ground.

He twisted around to face me, screaming in agony. I could have ended it before he'd even had the chance to turn around, but with the odds so heavily in our favour now, we are just playing with him a little before we decide to put him out of his misery.

I step backwards and laugh, just as he'd done at my expense only moments ago. Anger replaces the pain on his face and his right arm now lifts as he tries to use his remaining whip, but Petra quickly sees to it that his right arm meets the same fate as the left.

Dalip now buckles, falling to his knees and only just managing to stop his face from hitting the ground. As he heaves himself upwards and his head rises to meet my gaze, his face was a picture of shock and disbelief.

I sheath one of my swords, then gripping the remaining one two-handed, I swing it ferociously through his neck, sending his head spinning high into the air before bouncing across the hall floor. His torso falls to ground with a thump.

Petra stands staring at me with that smouldering look of hers, her lips slowly arcing into a smile.

I stare back into her beautiful green eyes as the same smile begins to form on my own face.

We'd done it. Cero and the other Gods were done with forever. No longer did we need to worry about anyone else, the world was ours to do what we wanted with and yet, only twenty-four hours ago, I could never have predicted things working out in the manner in which they have.

Only when Petra began to whisper the truth of what was going on, into my ear the previous evening did we begin to plot and plan our own ending to Cero's plan.

Of course, I was a little hurt to find out that Petra getting close to me was initially under the orders of Cero. However, his plan did not include sleeping with me and falling in love. Both of which Petra has done of her own accord and when I look deep into her eyes, I believe her. When you truly love someone and spend so much time together intimately, I believe you learn to know when they are telling the truth or not. Hence, it did not take long for me to forgive her and move on and begin plotting Cero and the other Gods downfall.

Sure, I may have ended the hero worship I once had amongst the human race, but I can live with that. I don't need to be liked, but I will be feared and respected, and that is all I need to rule over them and ensure we keep the darker side of humanity from rearing its ugly head.

'The rule of the Gods is over!' I finally say.

'Am I not still a God?' Petra asks, petting her lip slightly.

'You were never really a God, none of you were. But you can be a Queen. My Queen!' I reply.

Petra walks towards me and we embrace, kissing passionately, before she takes my hand and leads me over to the windowed area.

'Look out there at it all,' she says with a sultry smile. 'It's all ours to rule as we see fit, King Jacob!'

King Jacob! Now that's got a nice ring to it. The rule of the Gods is over. Today marks the dawn of a new era for Earth and its civilisation. The dawn of King Jacob and Queen Petra.

All hail the King!

Other titles available from Alan Hotchkiss

The Other Side Trilogy

Book 1 – The Other Side

Book 2 – Revenge of the Queen

Book 3 – Black Death

Printed in Great Britain
by Amazon

16022111R00160